MEMORIES RESTORED

DISARRAY
BOOK TWO

JESSIE CAL

Copyright © 2016 by Jessie Cal

All rights reserved.

No part of this book may be reproduced in any form or by any electronic or mechanical means, including information storage and retrieval systems, without written permission from the author, except for the use of brief quotations in a book review.

❦ Created with Vellum

CHAPTER 1

A sliver of sunlight illuminated the dark island as I ran along the shoreline; the sand damp and hard. The December wind was piercing as it hit my face. I reached the rocky arch completely out of breath then glanced at my watch—another record broken, but it was still not fast enough. Field agents were trained. If I couldn't be as strong as them, I would have to be faster. Much faster.

I wiped the sweat off my forehead, still gasping for air. I slapped the brown hair from my face then glanced over my shoulder at a small cave behind me. I didn't hear any noise, but still, I watched it for a few seconds. There was no change. It was the same as it had been for weeks—dark and empty. I tried suppressing the paranoia and looked out to the ocean, sucking in the cold winter breeze. It helped a little, but I couldn't shake off the feeling that we still weren't safe.

I focused on the beach, the dark blue water, and thin white sand. I closed my eyes and smelled the salt in the air.

The birds had already begun to sing as the tip of the sun peeked over the horizon, bathing the sky a soft shade of blue.

It had been five weeks since we arrived in Fort Valley Island which was located just off the coast of California—and that was where we'd been stuck ever since. It wasn't that we couldn't leave the island, it was that we shouldn't. The only one who went once a week was Dr. Dale and his wife, but only to buy groceries and other necessities.

Dale used to work with Dr. Jin, until the Order—the leaders of the Catalyst trial—found out Jin was keeping a record of all of the glitches in the trial. As well as all the illegal procedures done on the soldiers without their consent. Dr. Jin was going to turn it all into the N.I.M.H—National Institute of Mental Health—which fell under the H.H.S—Health and Human Services. Had Dr. Jin been able to carry out his plan, the Catalyst trial would've been shut down overnight. Dale was helping Dr. Jin, but when he was killed, Dale joined Rashida's team—fearing for his own life—and agreed to help her take down the Order.

"How many laps today?"

I turned around, and Hugh was walking up with his hands inside the pockets of his navy blue scrubs--that was all we had at the bunker.

"Two," I said, still out of breath. "I'm hoping to get three soon."

"Pace yourself," he warned, running his hands over his wavy black hair. "What was your timing?"

"An hour and twenty-three minutes."

"That's pretty fast."

"Not fast enough." I sat on a rock, exhausted from

running—for my life, that is. "How much longer do we have to stay here?"

"Hopefully, not much at all," Hugh said, hopeful. "Rashida and Benji finally located the Catalyst trial's external drive. Now, it's just a matter of figuring out how to get it."

"What will that do?"

"It'll give us proof of the glitches in the trial."

"And then?"

"We show it to the H.H.S," he said, making it sound so simple.

"Why can't we just take one of the soldiers to the H.H.S and let them see it for themselves?"

Hugh shook his head. "As soon as we get that soldier, all of his records will be wiped clean. We won't be able to prove he was ever part of the military. Unless we get the external drive, then we get all the records."

It was a solid plan, I wasn't arguing that, but they'd been going around in circles for five weeks. "How is Sophia doing?" I asked.

Hugh sighed. "Same. Still stressing about Mr. Jackson's contract and her boutique falling apart."

"I'm glad you both finally worked things out, though." I nudged him with my shoulder, and he smiled. "I don't know if I could bear seeing you drool over her a second longer."

He laughed. "Oh, trust me. Me either."

"What about Victor?" I asked. "How is he handling everything?"

"Victor's fine." Hugh looked at me, his green eyes soft and gentle. "You're the one I'm worried about. We all are."

I pushed myself up from the rock, hoping he would leave it alone but he stood with me.

"You hardly get any sleep. You spend all your time out here training. You keep to yourself most of the day and isolate everyone else. What's going on, Mia?"

I looked away. I didn't want him to see the grief that still lingered in my eyes. "I'm fine."

"No, you're not. Mia, look at me." Hugh waited, but I didn't turn around. "If you don't wanna talk to me, that's fine. But you have to talk to somebody. Rashida said—"

"I've had enough shrink sessions," I snapped.

Hugh put a comforting hand on my shoulder. "Then talk to me. You know I'm here for you."

We heard a boat in the distance, and I turned around with my heart racing.

"It's okay," Hugh said, raising a hand. "It's just Dale and his wife. They left last night. We were running short on a few things."

The boat pulled close to the rocks that went out to the ocean like a pier. Hugh and I climbed on the rocks and hopped over to where the boat docked. Dale's lack of hair made the top of his head glisten in the sun as he swung open a small door and rolled out a metal ramp toward us. Anne, his wife, stood next to him with her long silver hair. She smiled at us as Hugh caught the end of the ramp and pulled it out as far as it would go. Once it stopped, he lowered the ramp onto the rock while I reached under it for the side rails. I pulled it out on both sides then clicked it upward.

"Were you both okay out there?" Hugh asked over the loud sound of the engine.

"Pretty smooth," Dale responded, locking the ramp in place.

Hugh climbed first, meeting Dale halfway to grab the first few bags of groceries. I walked behind him and grabbed a few more. Dale and his wife managed the rest, and we all returned to the laboratory located in the middle of the island.

Once inside, I followed Dale's wife to the break room. "Where do you want these?" I asked without waiting for her to look at me. Of course, she didn't hear me. She was deaf. I kept forgetting. I stepped in front of her and showed her the bags. She smiled and pointed to the top of the counter.

"Here?" I asked.

She nodded.

I offered one of the few signs I knew. I placed the tip of my fingers to my chin and motioned outward. Thank you.

She smiled.

I knew I could've said it since she read lips, but she always seemed appreciative of anyone's efforts to sign. Victor had learned a lot more than me—probably because he was bored more often. All I'd learn was please, thank you, and I'm sorry. Though she was able to understand everyone, I felt bad that no one else other than her husband was able to understand her.

Dale walked in with Hugh, chatting about the latest update. Dale's wife turned to him and started signing. Dale nodded then turned to us.

"She'll make omelets for breakfast."

Hugh stepped in front of her. "Thank you," he said with a kind smile.

I slapped his arm. "This is how you say thank you." I showed him the sign.

He gave me a skeptical look. "Since when do you sign?"

"Since Dale's been teaching me."

"Dale, my man!" Victor walked in with long arms wide. "Did you get it? Please, tell me you got it."

Dale suppressed a laugh, picking up a step stool from the floor.

"Awesome!" Victor's brown eyes glowed. "Oh, it's perfect. Thanks, man." Victor turned to me and raised a hand in my direction. "Don't. I know what you're gonna say."

"Don't do it."

"I'm not listening." Victor walked out, managing to cover at least one of his ears. "Rash is gonna love it!"

Hugh came to stand next to me, shaking his head. "You gotta tell me how that goes."

"Oh, I don't even wanna be near it."

Hugh laughed. "Alright, Imma go wake Sophia." He touched my arm, his expression soft as ever. "Please, think about it."

I sighed, knowing he was referring to the conversation we had earlier at the beach. Maybe he was right, talking to someone could help. "Fine."

He gave my arm a friendly squeeze then walked out. I headed to the conference room where I found Rashida with her head down, her puffy black hair pulled up into a ponytail, and her eyes glued to the computer screen.

"Mia, guess what?" She lifted her eyes with a wide grin. "Benji was able to hack into the Catalyst trial system last night!"

I walked around to look at the screen. "Really?"

"Yes, but we can't connect while the main lab is connected," she explained. "We can only get in when they're closed. Isn't it great, though? If we have access to their system, we can get our hands on everything related to the trial."

"The glitches, too?"

"No, not that. But..." She raised a hopeful finger. "We have something better." She pointed to the computer screen. "You see this? One click here, and we could have years' worth of military training uploaded into our brain in minutes."

"Is that why they wanted to use the Catalyst in the military?"

"Not at first," she said. "All they wanted was to erase the soldiers' memories as they would come back from combat. They wanted the soldiers to get up the next morning, ready to keep fighting—no time for trauma. Which wasn't working, obviously, but anyway. It wasn't until the Order got their hands on Alice's journal—or at least the pages they took from you—that they found out about the anamnesis mode."

"So because of the anamnesis mode, they're now able to insert military training into the minds of the soldiers?"

"Exactly. Have you seen videos of them training?" She almost sounded envious. "They are ridiculously in sync. I mean, flawless. You have to see it, Mia. It's perfection."

"How does that help us in getting the external drive?" I asked, hoping for a connection.

"I don't know, yet. But check this out." She looked around, searching for something. Her eyes fell on a newspaper on top of the cabinet. "Are you serious?" She walked to the corner and grunted as she jumped on the table, reaching for it with the tips of her small fingers. "Come on!" She flicked it, and when it fell, she caught it with a proud smile. "Okay, so..." She jumped down and handed me a page from the newspaper. "This is the new president. It turns out he hasn't been told anything about the Catalyst trial. Once the H.H.S finds out about the surges and seizures, they will contact the white house directly and shut the whole thing down."

"Why hasn't he been told about it?" I asked, examining the president's smiling face as he waved from the podium in the black and white picture.

"He probably wouldn't approve of it," Rashida said. "I've read a lot of positive things about him. He hates the war and can't wait to put an end to it."

"Who's been calling the shots, then?"

Rashida pointed to the picture, again. A man was standing next to him. He seemed to be glaring at the president. "That's the vice president. He was at the presentation during the fundraiser. The one you came to with Hugh. He was the one who gave the idea to the previous president to hire NeuroCorp to have the Catalyst trial used on the soldiers in the military base."

"Did he know about the surges?"

"Absolutely. As soon as they approached us with the idea, I told them everything." Rashida shook her head. "But they went ahead with it, anyway."

I threw the paper on top of the table and looked at her. "So, how close are we to getting the evidence we need?"

"Let me think on it some more," she said. "I'll come up with something, soon. I promise."

"Hey, Rash…" Victor walked in with the step stool in his hand, and I couldn't help but shake my head. "I got you something."

Rashida went back to typing in the computer, treating Victor like an annoying fly on the wall. But he sat on the table next to the laptop and held up the step stool in front of her face—blocking her view.

"For you, my lady."

She stopped and looked at it. "Is that a—"

"Step stool?" Victor flashed her a proud smile. "Yep. Just for you. Now, you don't have to be hopping up on things like a frog."

She stood up straighter and glared at him. She turned on her heel and stomped out of the room without saying a word.

Victor looked at me. "Did you see that? She loved it so much; she was at a loss for words."

I laughed. "I don't think that's what happened."

"Of course it was," he said, putting the stool on the floor. "Didn't you see how intense she stared me down? It was like she was undressing me with her eyes."

I laughed, pushing him toward the door. "We gotta have your head checked."

Archer peeked his head inside the room, and the humor suddenly vanished. Yes, my father, out of all people, was also on the island.

"Breakfast is ready," he said, still unsure how to interact with me.

Ditto.

* * *

IN THE BREAKROOM, I stood in the food line next to Victor. It wasn't a large room, but there were only nine of us—Archer, Hugh, Sophia, Dale, his wife, Rashida, Benji, Victor and me.

"How do I look?" Victor asked in a hushed tone, glancing over his shoulder at Rashida who was standing with Archer and Benji, ahead of us. "Should I brush it to the right or the left?"

"I don't think she cares."

"Of course she does," he snorted. "Besides, today is the day. I'm ready to take our relationship to the next level."

"Does Rashida even know she's in a relationship with you?"

"Oh, she knows..." He cocked his head and brushed his hair to the right. "She just doesn't want to admit it. But that won't be a problem for long. I mean, look at me. How could she resist this?"

I laughed and pushed him forward. "Let's go, Casanova. I'm hungry."

After picking up our plates, Victor and I sat across from Sophia who was sketching in a notebook. Hugh sat next to her.

"So, how did your dad end up here, anyway?" Victor asked, his mouth full of toast. Archer was sitting with Rashida, Benji, Dale and his wife on another table.

"After he got out of rehab, he heard about Ethan and Shawn," Hugh replied. "Then, when Mia was nowhere to be found, he knew right away it had to do with the journal. So, he started snooping around in the NeuroCorp computer at the library where he worked. Lucky for him, it was Rashida who caught him."

"Did she tell him where Mia was?" Sophia asked, looking up from her sketchbook and pinning her black hair with a pencil.

"She just told him Mia was somewhere safe. Then, invited him to join the group."

"Small world, huh?" Victor said with a light chuckle. "So, why is it that you don't get along with your dad?"

I glanced at Archer, and he looked away. "Long story."

Victor was just about to take a bite of his muffin when he jerked back. "Whoa!" He tipped over his juice, and it spilled toward Sophia.

"Watch it, you moron!" She lifted her sketchbook quickly, but it was too late. The liquid caught almost half of the page. "God, Victor!"

"Sorry." Victor threw his hands in the air. "There are peanuts in this."

"I don't care!" She pushed him away then reached for a napkin. "You're such an idiot!" she grumbled, wiping the juice off her scrubs.

"I'm allergic to peanuts!"

"Whatever! You didn't have to jump like that."

Once Sophia noticed everyone was listening to their argument and looking at her, she made a frustrated sound and stormed out the door.

Hugh stood to follow, but I put a hand on his shoulder. "I'll go."

* * *

OUTSIDE, Sophia was sitting on a bench made of rocks about ten feet from the edge of the cliff, looking out to the ocean. Her black hair was pulled up in a ponytail. The wind was strong and cold, so I pulled my long hair back too, and zipped up my jacket.

I sat next to her and looked out to the horizon. "You're starting to feel it too, huh?"

She let out a frustrated sigh. "Why does it seem like I'm the only one going out of my mind?"

"You're not the only one. Trust me."

"Then why does everyone keep looking at me like I'm a ticking time bomb?" She turned to look at me, her eyes watering. "Have I been that bad?"

"We're all doing the best we can."

She buried her face in her hands and started to cry. "I miss him, Mia." She looked up with her green eyes, ashamed. "I don't want to, but I can't help it. Despite everything, he's still my dad." She choked a little. "And my mom...I miss her more than anything. I want my life back."

So did I, except there was no way that would ever happen for me. Even if we did get to shut down the Catalyst trial, it still wouldn't bring back my brother or my husband. I didn't even know what my mother looked like, so I couldn't go looking for her. Nothing would ever be the same for me, and my heart squeezed tight in my chest. Of course, I didn't tell Sophia any of that. She was distressed enough over her own anxieties.

I put a comforting hand on her shoulder. "You will get your life back. I'm sure of it."

She wiped the tears off her cheeks and turned to look at

me. "What about you? What are you gonna do after all this is over?"

"I haven't thought about it, yet."

She offered a small smile. "You can keep working with me if you like. Unless you think that would be too weird now that I'm with Hugh."

"Oh, please. If I got a penny for every time he talked about you; I would be richer than you, right now."

Sophia blushed, wiping what was left of her tears.

"I'm serious. It was pretty pathetic."

She nudged me with her shoulder, a shy smile forming on her lips.

"I promise you, friend." I reached for her hand and looked her in the eyes. "Hugh will never be anything more than just a brother to me. And it makes me so happy to see you both finally working it out."

"Hugh told me about Ethan," she said, her voice soft, almost careful. "He told me you were crazy for him."

"Yeah... literally." I chuckled, remembering how he had been a figment of my imagination the whole time my memories were gone.

"Have you been able to see him again?" she asked.

"Not since I got my memories back," I said with a heavy heart. "But that's okay. Maybe it's for the best."

Sophia turned to face me with a glow in her eyes. "What was he like?"

"Oh..." I gazed out to the horizon. Such a simple question, yet I had no idea where to even begin. "He was funny, kind, considerate, but also very crazy." I laughed, remembering how he did a backflip off the edge of the waterfall. "He was so much fun, though."

Sophia smiled. "Tell me about it."

"Hmm… what if I show you?"

"Okay."

I jumped up, grabbed her hand, and pulled her to the edge of the cliff. "Let's jump."

"What?" She ripped her hand away from me and stepped back. "That's a twenty-foot drop!"

"We got sneakers on. We'll be fine."

She looked down to the bottom. "Is that even safe?"

"I've jumped several times with Ethan. Not here, but back home."

"I don't know—"

"Sophia." I offered her my hand. "Trust me."

She opened her mouth to debate, but then grumbled, "Fine." She took my hand and stepped back to stand next to me. "Are there rocks down there?"

"Not on this side."

She took a deep breath. "Okay."

"On the count of three," I warned, and she nodded. "One…" We swayed together. "Two…" We looked at each other, terrified. "Three!"

CHAPTER 2

*I*N THE CONFERENCE ROOM, Rashida leaned over her laptop at the end of the large oval table. Hugh sat across from Dale's wife. Dale stood to grab a bottle of water from the back. Archer sat close to Rashida, his face still buried in the same thick psychology textbook he'd been carrying around for the past few days.

Benji pushed up his glasses then brought the projector to the center of the conference table. He whispered something to Rashida as he connected it to her laptop.

Sophia and I made our way to the back where Victor was swinging back on his chair with his foot propped up on the table.

"Where were you?" Victor whispered.

"We went cliff diving," Sophia whispered back. "It was so insane!"

Victor crossed his arms, unamused. "And you didn't call me?"

"We were bonding. Now, move." Sophia shoved Victor's feet off the table and took a seat next to Hugh. Victor put his feet up on the table, again. "Get your feet out of my face—"

"Enough, you two." I pushed my chair between the bickering siblings, and they fell silent. "Why are we here, anyway?" I asked Hugh.

"Your guess is as good as mine," he said with a shrug.

"So, listen up," Rashida said, moving from her face her puffy black hair which rested just above her shoulders. "We have finally come up with a plan."

I sat up straight in my seat, intrigued.

She signaled for Benji to turn off the lights while Archer pointed the projector to the wall. The image it showed was a picture of the blueprint for the NeuroCorp Headquarters.

"So, the external drive with all sealed records are in a vault at the NeuroCorp Headquarters," Rashida said, pointing to the picture from the projector. "We would go in through the vents, take out whatever guards are in these sections over here, get into the vault which is underground, then get out through the west wing."

"Wait," Hugh shook his head, trying to understand. "You want us to break into their Headquarters?"

"How many guards are we talking about?" I asked, willing to do whatever it takes. Anything would be better than hiding.

"It's hard to say how many we'll actually encounter," Rashida said, pointing to the red dots all throughout the blueprint. "But total, we're looking at about…seventy, maybe more."

"Oh! Don't forget the male nurses," Benji added from the corner of the room.

"Right." Rashida clicked again, and blue dots appeared in the picture, making the building look even more infested. "Although they're not necessarily armed, they do carry Tasers."

"Okay." Sophia stood, pushing her chair back with the back of her legs. "I may be slow when it comes to all of this but let me see if I understand this correctly. So, you expect the nine of us," she pointed around the small, crowded room, "to go against an army of them," she pointed to the projector's reflection on the wall, "steal the most compromising evidence they own and still walk out of there in one piece?"

"Technically... five of us." Rashida pointed around the room. "We need Benji to stay behind with the computer and be our eagle eye. We can't communicate with Dale's wife, and Dale will stay with her. As for Archer, well, we need him alive in case we don't make it out."

Sophia stared at Rashida with the most stupid plan expression she could muster.

"I know." Rashida lifted a finger with an excited grin. "But it can be done. Archer?" She signaled to Archer, and he hesitantly took her place in front of the group. He didn't seem comfortable being the center of attention, and I wondered how in the world he was ever a professor.

Archer signaled Benji to turn the lights back on. "This is actually quite interesting," he started, looking around the room. "As of last night, we now have at our disposal the entire military training data."

Rashida squealed in excitement. "Sorry. Go on."

Sophia looked at me then rolled her eyes. She couldn't stand Rashida.

"With this new feature," Archer continued, "the Catalyst machine is able to insert full military training directly into a person's mind. It's as easy as uploading information into a computer. Now, they don't have to waste so much time actually training them on what to do but instead spend more time training them on how to do it."

"How does that work, exactly?" Hugh asked, sitting back and lacing his long fingers together. Sophia reached for his hand, and he held it in his.

"Well, let's say the military wants to train a person to skydive. They will first spend months learning everything there is to know about skydiving, then—and only then—can they actually start to physically train for it. But by inserting the military training into their minds, they don't have to hit the books anymore. They just have to train their bodies physically on how to use the information."

Victor smiled. "I wouldn't mind trying that."

Sophia slapped him.

"What?" he grumbled. "Sounds pretty cool."

"You are not getting in that machine," she hissed.

"We appreciate your enthusiasm, but we're going to take things slow," Archer said, looking at Victor. "Rashida has already volunteered to have the military training inserted into her first. We will study and monitor her to see what effects can be expected, and if everything goes smoothly, we'll go ahead and insert it on everyone else."

As useful as the whole military training sounded, I couldn't picture myself ever being put through that machine again.

"Even if the insertion works," Hugh added. "Won't we still need a lot more people for this plan to work?"

Where in the world would we get more people?

"If our small group trains well," Archer said, "it's possible we could make it."

"And if we don't?" Hugh asked, even though I couldn't imagine he didn't already know the answer.

Archer rubbed the back of his neck. "Then, we don't."

Sophia leaned over to me, her voice low. "What did he mean by that?" Her eyes were stretched wide, and I could tell she understood what he'd meant, but was looking for some type of reassurance. Or perhaps, hoping to be wrong.

"We get caught and have our memories wiped."

* * *

RASHIDA and I crouched in a thick underbrush on the north side of the island. A mosquito came annoyingly close to my ear, but I knew better than to swat it away. Rashida insisted I remain perfectly still. It had already been a week since we began training. Though only Rashida had the actual military insertion in her mind, we all trained with her.

"Do you see it?" Rashida whispered. "It's right there."

I followed her gaze up a tall tree and squinted through bright beams of sunlight that shined through the leaves. "I don't see anything."

Rashida's eyes were focused. "I see it."

Before I could reply, she darted forward and climbed the tree with such swiftness and agility I could barely keep myself from gaping.

"How did you do that?" I asked in disbelief.

A heavy hand slammed into my back.

"Gotcha!" Victor exclaimed.

Rashida hung onto the branches while clinging to a white makeshift flag made from one of Victor's t-shirts.

"She's not the one with the flag," Rashida said.

"Either way, she's out." Victor looked up at her and smiled. "And you'll have to come down at some point."

Rashida looked out across the horizon as the sun began to set. She didn't appear fazed, despite how high she was off the ground. It must have been a side effect from the implant, a soldier showing no fear.

"I could stay up here forever," Rashida said, closing her eyes.

Victor crept closer to the tree and slowly began to climb the protruding branches. A flimsy wooden limb cracked under his weight. Rashida opened her eyes and flashed him a devious smile. She flung herself out of the dense foliage, grabbed an adjacent tree, and slid down the trunk. I cringed at the sound of her nails scraping against the bark, but Rashida didn't flinch. Her feet hit the ground with a heavy thud, and she took off running.

Victor's jaw dropped. He jumped down and charged after her. I quickly followed behind, my heart beating hard against my chest as I dodged rock masses and uneven tree stumps. Off in the distance, Hugh leaped out from his hiding spot and closed in on Rashida.

"On your right!" I yelled.

Rashida glanced over her shoulder and veered left, just out of Hugh's reach. The two men pushed themselves harder, sweat beading down their foreheads, but they could not match her speed. She raced across an invisible line into a small clearing—her home base.

Rashida raised the tattered white flag above her head and let out a triumphant cry. "I win!" Her voice echoed throughout the island.

Sophia stood nearby with her arms folded across her chest. She had been out for most of the game.

"Yes, yes, we know you're fast." Sophia flicked dirt from her shoulders. "Are we done?"

The three of us stumbled into the clearing, barely able to catch our breath. My legs felt like they were on fire.

"You know Rash," Victor said, straightening his posture. "If you ever want to take my shirt from me, just say the word, and I won't make you work so hard for it." He winked at her, and she pushed him down into a puddle of mud.

"Stop calling me Rash," she hissed as she walked away.

"Wow." Victor laughed as he crawled out of the mud. "You put a whole new meaning to the word dirty. I like it!"

"Stop being an idiot." Sophia kicked his leg. "Get up and go shower. You stink."

"I'm sure when you run for three hours, you smell like flowers," Victor said, sarcastically.

Sophia walked away, ignoring her brother.

* * *

AFTER I FINISHED MY SHOWER, I headed back to the room I shared with Rashida. She was pacing around with a bag of peanuts in her hand. She seemed to be deep in concentration.

"You okay?" I asked, drying my hair with a towel.

"According to my fitness tracker, I only need two

hundred more steps to reach twenty thousand." She smiled, lifting her wristband. "Almost there."

"Twenty thousand? Wow. I didn't realize how much running we did today. Where's everybody? It was pretty quiet out there."

"Hugh went to shower. Sophia is sketching in her room. Dale and his wife went out for a walk. Your dad and Benji are doing more research. As for Victor…" She pretended to choke on a peanut and made a gagging sound. "I honestly couldn't care less."

I laughed.

Rashida's tracker finally buzzed, and she sat on the edge of her bed. "So, we stumbled on some new info. Turns out the Order has discovered how to create illusions to play as memories and insert those into a person's mind."

"Illusions?"

"Yep." She kept throwing her peanuts in the air and catching with her mouth. "They upload the real memory into a simulator and tamper with them."

"What do you mean, temper?"

"They add things that were never there. Things that never even existed. It's almost impossible for the subject to differentiate between what's real and what's not. And that's if they decide to keep any of the real memories, at all."

"Wow. How have they been using that?"

"I'm not sure. They don't have any records." Rashida stopped eating and looked at me, her expression suddenly serious. "I don't think I ever apologized to you, by the way. It's probably been implied, but I still wanted to say it. I'm sorry for everything we put you through. And for lying to you."

"I know you guys were just looking out for me."

"For what is worth, I did try to get Hugh to tell you the truth."

I waved it off. "That's all behind us now. So, tell me. How's the military training, so far?" I hung the towel on the closet door then grabbed my hairbrush. "Anything unusual?"

"Overall, it's been incredible." Her eyes widened in excitement. "I feel so different but in a good way. Like, smart and powerful and...so much more. I don't even know how to describe it."

I studied her for a second. "Overall?"

"Yeah, well..." She sighed. "Nothing's perfect, right?"

"What's wrong?"

"I'm not sure." She stood and started pacing, again. "Tell me something. When you used to have those surges...what did they feel like, exactly? Was it like a strong headache?"

"It was a lot stronger than a headache. It felt like my head was going to explode. I mean, I had a seizure, remember?"

"Yeah, but did they all feel like that?"

"Pretty much. Although, some didn't last as long."

She nodded, intrigued. "Interesting."

"Why are you asking all of this?" I gave her a skeptical look. "What side effects are you having?"

She shook her head. "I'm honestly not sure. I just know that sometimes I don't feel like myself." She sat back down. "It's as if something shuts off in my brain and I do things without thinking or feeling. I don't know how to explain it."

"Have you told Archer?"

"Yes." She raised her fitness tracker. "That's why he connected me to this. It monitors my pulse, heart rate, and brain waves. They're looking into it as we speak."

"You could remove the military training, you know?"

"It's too soon to give up on it." She went back to throwing her peanuts in the air. "Besides, every trial has its risks, and somebody's gotta take 'em."

"Is that Rashida talking or the new soldier in you?"

She shrugged. "Both, I guess." She smiled then offered me her peanut bag. "Want some?"

"No, thanks."

"Alright, then." She started toward the door. "Imma go check in with Archer. Oh, by the way!" She swung back on her heel. "You might want to knock some sense into Hugh. He's been asking me for a new identity so he can go off— God knows where. Apparently, he has a plan. I don't know. It sounds stupid to me. Maybe, he'll listen to you."

As Rashida turned around to leave, Victor jumped out of the closet next to the front door, and Rashida ripped a screeching yelp. I bounced back, my heart drumming in my chest. Suddenly, a strong shock wave stung my brain, and I buried my face into my pillow, waiting for the pain to subside. It felt like a surge, but there was no trigger with it.

As the pain began to wean, I opened my eyes and noticed Rashida was also holding her head. But then she opened her eyes and glared at Victor. "You..." She growled as she grabbed him by his shirt and pinned him to the wall.

"I'm sorry, Rash!" Victor spoke through his laughter. "That scare wasn't meant for you. I hid in here to wait for Mia but then you came in, and I was gonna tell you I was in there, but then I thought, Wait! What if she changes in here? I would love to see some of that! But then nothing happened, and you were just so close. I couldn't help it." He was still laughing, and she slammed him against the wall. "Wow, you're strong."

"And you're a pervert!" she yelled.

"Oh, c'mon!" He cocked his head. "You're gonna tell me you wouldn't love to see me in my briefs?"

Suddenly, something changed about Rashida's demeanor and her lips lifted into a wicked smile. "You know what?" she spoke in a much softer tone. "You're right."

Victor froze. "I am?"

Rashida loosened her grip and smoothed his shirt. "You know what else I would love to do right now?" Before he could reply, she pulled him down and kissed him on the lips.

I stared at them agape, but it wasn't until I saw her tongue go into his mouth that I hurried out the door. I shut it quickly behind me and stood there, speechless.

What in the world was that? I shook my head, feeling weird—numb of any feeling or emotion. Being stuck on this island was driving everyone out of their minds.

Including Hugh, apparently.

I marched toward the locker room. Ignoring all boundaries of privacy, I barged into the men's shower room and stomped toward the only shower that was turned on. Without any hesitation, I pushed the curtain to the side.

Hugh jumped back, startled. "What in the world…!" He reached for a towel and wrapped it around his waist. "Mia, what are you doing?"

"Are you out of your mind?" I entered into the shower

with him and pinned him against the wall. My face only mere inches from his. The shower was drenching us both, and he looked at me like I was crazy.

"What's gotten into you? And why are your eyes pitch black?"

"Do you wanna get killed?" I snapped. "Why would you even consider leaving?"

"Can we talk about this somewhere else—"

"No."

"Mia—"

"You're not leaving!"

"I have a plan," he said. "I have a contact at the military base in Fort Knox. His name is Seth. He's already getting a group of soldiers together."

"Fort Knox?" I echoed. "They are going to slaughter you!"

"I have everything under control."

"No!"

"Mia, what's gotten into you?"

"I'm not losing you, too!"

Hugh fell silent and his gaze softened. Water was getting in my eyes, but I blinked them away. "Mia, you're not going to lose me."

I pushed his chin up with my forearm. "Then stop being an idiot."

Sophia's gasp made Hugh's body tense.

"What's going on?" she asked, her voice in pure shock. "Mia?"

I pulled away from Hugh, still irritated. "Knock some sense into this idiot. I'm done." I left them two to handle their issues and grabbed a dry towel on the way out.

On my way down the hall, I felt lightheaded and leaned against the wall. I shook my head, something felt off. My brain stung, and at that moment it dawned on me what I'd just done. I pulled at my drenched scrubs as it stuck to my skin. What in the world came over me?

"Whoa, M's..." Victor stopped in front of me. "What happened?"

"I'm not sure." I looked up at him, still in a daze. But then I saw that he had rashes on his face and arms. "What happened to you?"

"Oh, I'll tell you what happened." He pulled off his shirt and his whole body was covered in rashes, even up to his neck.

"Is that...?"

"An allergic reaction? Yes! I'm allergic to peanuts, and umpa lumpa over there was eating peanuts when she kissed me!" he paused then crossed his arms. "And you know what she said to me? Who's rash now?"

My head began to spin, and I grabbed onto the wall. Victor leaned forward and held my arm. "Are you alright, M's?"

"Yeah," I mumbled, fighting what felt like vertigo. "I just need some fresh air."

Outside, the breeze felt cool, and the sky was as dark as I'd ever seen. The sound of cicadas filled the air as I followed the trail down to the beach. I stepped on the cold soft sand, and the full moon was bright as it reflected off the water. There were tons of stars too, but I wasn't in that kind of mood. I made my way to the rocky arch and started the timer.

* * *

BY THE TIME I finished running, the sun was starting to rise. I crossed the arch panting and out of breath, sweat dripping down the side of my face, and I could no longer feel my legs. I collapsed on the sand, overwhelmed by exhaustion.

I glanced toward the cave. It was still empty, and I felt a tightness in my chest. "How come you don't show yourself, anymore?" I whispered as tears blurred my vision. "Please... I need to see you. Please, come back. I'll do anything." I clawed at my chest, something felt stuck in my heart. "Ethan, please."

"Oh, Mia."

I turned around, blinking the tears away. "Ethan?"

The shadow stepped into the light, and my heart sank. It was Hugh.

"No..." There was an earthquake in my chest, and I doubled over sobbing, wrapping my arms around my torso, trying to hold myself together. Hugh rushed to my side and wrapped his arms around me.

"Oh, it hurts..." I couldn't breathe. "Hugh, it hurts." I clung to his arm, trying to find some sort of steadiness. "Oh, God. I miss him so much." I pressed at my chest to try in stop the bleeding. "He's gone, Hugh. He's really gone."

Hugh tightened his arms around me. "I'm sorry."

"I can't lose you too," I cried, burying my face into his chest. "You're the only family I have left. I can't bear it. Please, don't go."

"I won't." There was pain in his voice. "I promise."

I looked up at him, and when our eyes met, I knew he

was telling the truth. He cocked his head and wiped the tears off my cheeks.

"I should've known that's why you were isolating yourself," he said, brushing a strand of hair from my face. "Why didn't you tell me?" He sat next to me and tightened his arms around me. "I'm here for you. That's never gonna change, you hear me?"

I nodded, feeling a weight lifted off of me. I closed my eyes, giving in to the exhaustion, but was suddenly jolted with Sophia letting out a horrified scream from the top of the cliff. Hugh and I both jumped to our feet, startled. Something heavy splashed into the water and Hugh and I looked at each other.

"Victor!" Sophia cried.

We ran toward the ocean but then froze when we saw Victor's body floating and the water around him turning red. I gasped. Hugh jumped in the water with his shoes on, there were too many rocks on that side of the cliff. I looked up, and Rashida was on her knees frozen in shock with her mouth hanging open.

"Mia, help me!" Hugh called out trying to keep his head above the crashing waves as he struggled to bring Victor back to shore. I ran into the water and grabbed onto Victor's legs, while Hugh carried him by the arms.

"His leg is bleeding!" I said, horrified. "His head, too!"

We laid Victor down on the hard sand. Hugh ripped part of his pants and wrapped it around Victor's head, putting pressure on it. I did the same with my scrubs and wrapped it tight around his leg.

"He needs to go to a hospital," I said, my hands shaking.

"Let's take him to Dale, first," Hugh said, hooking his

hands under Victor's arms. "Come on. Lift him up. Let's go."

On our way up the trail, Sophia hurried to meet us halfway. She was still crying as she called out Victor's name for the thousandth time, but it got worse once she noticed he wasn't responding. I sped up trying to keep up with Hugh's pace, though my arms kept wanting to give out. Hugh sped up some more, and my knees began to wobble. I sucked in a deep breath. Almost there.

Archer came out with a confused look, but then his eyes widened and he rushed to my side. "What happened?" he asked, taking Victor's weight onto himself. My body weakened as soon as Archer took over and I dropped to my knees.

"That maniac pushed Victor off the cliff!" Sophia pointed at Rashida who was watching us from a distance.

"I'm so sorry..." Rashida mumbled, but upon hearing her voice, Sophia charged in her direction. I staggered back to my feet and tackled Sophia before her nails reached Rashida's face.

"Let go of me!" Sophia tried squirming from under me. "I am going to kill her!"

"Sophia, stop!" I forced her to look at me. "Victor needs you right now. Go be with him."

I loosened my grip slowly, and she huffed. "Fine, but she's not getting anywhere near my brother!" Sophia pushed herself to her feet and rushed inside.

I turned to look at Rashida, and she started to cry.

CHAPTER 3

HUGH WAS SITTING with Sophia on the floor of the hallway outside Victor's room. Hugh had an arm around Sophia while she cried into his chest. Archer was seated across from them, rubbing his eyes.

"How is he doing?" I asked, sitting next to Archer. He looked at me surprised that I was talking to him. I tried to ignore it. "Is Dale still in there?"

"Yes," he responded, combing his fingers through his messy gray hair. "He hasn't come out, yet."

Hugh kissed Sophia on the forehead then whispered into her ear, "He's gonna be fine."

Sophia nodded, still crying.

"What happened out there?" I asked, and Sophia looked up—her eyes swollen red. "What did Rashida do, exactly?"

Sophia sucked in a breath, trying to control her temper as she heard Rashida's name. "That maniac wanted to do more training and Victor, as stupid as he is, offered to help. I didn't like the idea, but I also didn't want to be down here by myself. So, we headed to the cliff and when she leaned over to look down, Victor goofed around, pretending he was going to push her. Then..." Sophia began to raise her voice, "that lunatic grabbed him by his shirt and pushed him off the cliff! She could've killed him! She's insane!"

Archer brought a finger to his lips as he often did when he was thinking deeply about something. "When Victor pretended to push her off the cliff, did Rashida get scared?"

Sophia stared at Archer as if he was missing the point. "Who cares! My brother could've died!" Sophia started crying again, and Hugh pulled her into him.

Archer turned to me. "It doesn't make any sense," he whispered. "We're missing something."

Dale opened the door, and we all jumped to our feet. Dale turned to Sophia. "He broke a foot and a few ribs. He's going to be in a lot of pain, especially for the next few days, but in the long run...he should recover fully."

Sophia let out a cry of relief. "Can I see him?"

"Sure, but he won't be waking up anytime soon. The pain meds should keep him out for a while."

Sophia bolted past Dale and rushed to Victor's side.

"Thanks, Dale." Hugh shook his hand in a firm grip. "You have been a real asset to this team."

Dale waved it off. "Whatever I can do to help."

The TV finally came to life, and gasps filled the conference room. Dale turned around, surprised. "What was that?"

Archer went ahead, and we all followed after him. We gathered around the TV. It looked like a news report. "What is it?" I asked.

"It's an update on the war in China," Benji said, turning

up the volume. "That's footage of the aftermath of last night's invasion. The soldiers went totally insane and massacred tons of innocent people. Witnesses say they were completely out of control."

The TV showed piles and piles of dead bodies only a few feet behind the reporter as she presented the story in tears. The caps underneath read: *Hundreds of Chinese civilians massacred by American soldiers.*

"They're killing civilians?" Hugh grabbed a clipboard from the table and threw it against the wall, cursing under his breath. Benji switched off the TV, and no one moved or said anything for a long time.

I leaned over to Dale and his wife, who were leaning against the far back wall. "How is the Order responsible for that?" I whispered.

Dale shrugged. "I have no idea."

"I do," Archer said, turning on the projector that was connected to the computer. "Can someone please go get Rashida?"

"No need." Rashida walked in with her shoulders sagged and her eyes swollen red. She took a seat next to Benji, in the corner.

Hugh turned off the lights, and Archer looked up from the laptop. "We have been monitoring Rashida ever since we inserted the military training into her brain," he said, turning toward the chart projected on the wall. "The top chart shows her heart rate while the bottom chart shows her brain waves. Now..." he pointed to the middle of the chart, "can you see how her heart rate peaked right before she pushed Victor off the cliff?"

Rashida shrunk in her seat at the sound of Victor's name.

"Now, look at her brain waves." Archer pointed to the bottom chart. "See how it drops? Adrenaline normally doesn't do that to the brain. It does the opposite. It's supposed to rise along with the heart rate." He switched the slide to another chart with a bunch of numbers and codes and started to talk like the college professor he used to be.

"English, please," I cut in.

"Right, sorry. So, what I'm trying to say is...whenever Rashida's heart rate peaks passed a certain level, somehow that adrenaline rush causes her conscience to turn off. Like a dormant effect."

"Her conscience turned off?" Hugh echoed.

Archer nodded. "The moment she got scared, yes."

"But why would she push him off the cliff?" Hugh asked, turning to look at Rashida, whose eyes were widened like two fried eggs.

"Our conscience serves as a moral guide for our decisions," Archer explained. "Without it, we do things that otherwise we wouldn't do."

Hugh and I looked at each other, and I could tell he was wondering the same thing I was. Was that happening to me, too? It would explain why I barged into Hugh's shower without any hesitation.

"I think it might've been the insertion of the military training," Archer went on, and I had to force myself to focus. "That would explain what's happening to the soldiers, too. Killing civilians and all."

"Or..." I added, hesitantly. "It could've been the insertion itself."

Everyone's heads turned in my direction, they looked confused. "What makes you say that?" Archer asked.

"I think that dormant effect might've happened to me, too."

Archer's eyes widened. "What happened?"

"I attacked Hugh in the shower."

"The point is..." Hugh cut in, his face beet red. "How do we fix it?"

Archer nodded, though still studying me. "For starters, you should wear a wristband, too."

Benji pulled out a fitness tracker from a drawer and threw it to me.

"Now, as for fixing it..." Archer picked up a pile of paperwork and started shuffling through it. "I'm not sure. We followed the procedure step by step, just like they had it in the system. Just like they've been doing it on the trial."

"So, what can we do?" I asked.

Archer rubbed the back of his neck. "The only thing I can think of..." he paused but only for a moment, "is reversing the insertion."

"Reversing?" I echoed. "As in...removing my memories again?"

"Not all of the memories," Archer clarified, trying to sound optimistic. "Only the ones that have been inserted by us, in this facility."

"So..." Rashida cut in. "You would just remove the military training from my mind, and I would be okay?"

"In your case, yes," Archer said, but then looked at me, and all optimism was out the window. Not good. Not good, at all. "In Mia's case, however…" He didn't finish, but then again, he didn't have to.

"No way." I felt my heart drop in my chest. "You are not removing my entire life again."

"You would still be able to keep the last eight months—"

"You mean the fake life where I was married to Hugh? Absolutely not." The idea of forgetting Ethan again made it so hard to breathe. I stood and paced around the room. I couldn't do it. I would rather gamble with my conscience every day for the rest of my life than living a life without Ethan. I'd already lost him. The memories of him were all I had left. "I can't." My eyes began filling with tears. "I can't lose him again. I just can't."

Archer didn't respond.

No one did.

But then it occurred to me, and I stopped, sucking back the tears. "There is something else we can try." I looked at Rashida. "The missing pages."

CHAPTER 4

"ARE YOU ALRIGHT?" Rashida asked as I stared out the window of Dale's car.

We parked in front of the Bunker Hill Medical Center. That was the hospital where my brother had died. "Yeah, I'm fine." I pushed the thought away and forced myself to focus. I couldn't afford to be distracted. Not here. Not now.

"Ready?" Rashida reached for the handle.

I took a deep breath. "Let's go."

We jumped out the car and started toward the east wing.

"I thought you said you hid the loose pages somewhere else," Rashida spoke in a hushed tone as she followed me into the same restroom I'd hid the journal.

"I did," I said once we were inside the empty restroom. "I hid the journal under that counter but the loose pages, I shoved it in here." I jumped up on the counter and looked into the air conditioning vent. "Yep, it's still in there." I tried sticking my finger through the narrow opening, but they weren't thin enough. I couldn't even touch the Ziploc bag. "I can't reach it. Do you have a hair clip?"

Rashida pulled it out of her hair and handed it to me. "Hurry up."

There were four screws, one in each corner. I used the broader side of the clip to unscrewed one on the bottom and one on the top. I pulled out the vent, but it only stretched so far. "I'm touching it! I can feel it!" I reached in further. "Almost—"

"Oh..." a woman gasped as she stood by the door. "Hello?"

"Hi. Don't mind us," Rashida said, crossing her arms casually and leaning against the wall. "Just checking out the AC."

The woman looked up at me, then back at Rashida with her eyes widened in shock. We shouldn't seem too out of place; after all, we were wearing scrubs in a hospital.

"You ok?" Rashida asked.

The woman snapped out of it and forced a smile. "Sure. Yeah." She backed out in a hurry, and we could hear her heels clicking away like she was running.

"What was that about?" I wondered.

Rashida turned around and looked at the far wall behind us. "You have got to be kidding me!"

I glanced over my shoulder. There was a 'wanted' sign with our picture on it.

"How did they know we were coming?" Rashida ripped the picture off the wall and threw it in the gar-bage. "Mia, we have to hurry!"

I forced my hand into the narrow opening, scraping my

flesh against the textured wall and as soon as I felt the plastic brush the tip of my fingers, I pulled it out. "Got it!"

We strolled out of the restroom with an innocent look on our faces, but it quickly faded when we spotted the woman talking to one of the security guards and pointing in our direction.

Rashida grabbed me by my arm. "Run!"

"Stop!" the guard yelled, running after us. I shoved the Ziploc bag into my bra and sprinted toward the car.

The guard followed us out, speaking into his radio. Two cops were talking outside, but by the time they heard the guard, we were already by the car.

"Keys!" I raised my hand, and Rashida threw it to me. She jumped in the passenger seat and buckled her seat belt. I roared the engine to life, and the vibration of the steering wheel under my grip filled me with a nostalgic adrenaline I only got from racing.

Oh, how I missed it! I looked in the rearview mirror and watched as the cops jumped in their car and turned on their lights.

My lips lifted into a grin, and I firmed my grip on the steering wheel. Bring it on. I reversed out of the parking spot and stomped on the gas, screeching the tires on the cement. The cop did a poor imitation, and I laughed.

They didn't stand a chance.

* * *

I PARKED the car near the marina—since that was our only way back to the boat—and grabbed a cap from the backseat. Rashida shuffled through the glove compartment and found sunglasses. We stepped out of the car inconspicuously, but to no avail. Two men with dark aviator glasses picked up their pace as they crossed the parking lot.

"We got company," I said, trying not to move my lips. "And they don't look like cops."

"You're right," Rashida whispered back. "Check out their earpiece. They're definitely field agents."

"On my count, ready?"

Rashida nodded.

"Go!" I took off running to the left while Rashida followed suit to the right. I sprinted into the crowd and braced myself, bumping into people and stumbling over sea lions. I looked over my shoulder, and one of the two men was right at my tail.

I pushed my legs harder, but then I saw a child ahead. She couldn't have been older than three-years-old. She climbed out of her stroller and ran across the pier to touch a baby sea lion. The animal got scared and bumped her little legs, throwing her off balance. I gasped as I watched her wobble toward the water.

I sped up and grabbed the child's shirt, yanking her back. She ripped a terrified scream, and everyone turned to look. The parents hurried to aid their little girl as I fell to the ground.

As the parents took the girl into their arms, I chanced a look over their shoulders. I couldn't see anything past the crowd that started making a circle around the girl. I rolled myself into the water then surfaced underneath the pier. It was cold, and my legs began to shiver.

I peeked through the gaps of the wood and caught sight of my pursuer pushing and shoving everyone out of his way. He looked around, confused. He yanked off his glasses in a furious rage and cursed under his breath. When he went to the edge of the dock, I dove underwater. It was hard to see, but I swam as deep as I could. I stretched out my hands, hoping not to crash into a wooden beam or a sea lion.

I swam up for air only a couple of times before reaching the end of the pier. My lungs were throbbing, and I was running out of breath.

A heavy hand grabbed the heel of my foot, and I took off swimming out to the open water. A jet ski swerved by, and I ducked. The man's hand grabbed my foot again. I kicked as hard as I could, and he lost his grip. I pushed myself to swim faster but so did he. His arms were longer than mine, and the tip of his fingers kept brushing against the back of my leg—

"Gotcha!" Rashida snatched me out of the water, and we both fell to the floor of the boat. She staggered back to take control of the wheel. I grabbed onto the seat and pulled myself up, my legs shaky and weak. I looked toward the harbor and saw the field agent slapping the water in a rage.

Rashida blurted out a laugh, amazed at how we were able to pull it off. I couldn't even believe it myself.

"We did it!" She cheered. "So, where are the pages?" she asked, jumping up and down, excited. "Let me see! Let me see!"

I reached into my bra, but as my fingers touched the Ziploc bag, I gasped.

Rashida mirrored the horrified expression on my face. "What's wrong?" she asked.

I pulled the bag out slowly without answering her.

"No..." She put the boat on autopilot and reached for the bag. "No, no, no." Or at least, what was left of the bag.

"It must've ripped when I pulled it out from the vent." I sighed. "I'm sorry."

Rashida didn't respond. She just stared at the ripped bag with its drenched pages inside. The ink of the pen smudged everything, making the handwriting unreadable. Rashida took the pages out of the bag and spread them out to dry, but most of them were stuck together. She tried separating a few but they ripped apart in her hand, and I winced.

Rashida dropped to her knees and stared at it as if it had just died in her arms. "This was our only hope," she spoke under her breath. "Now we'll never know how to fix these glitches."

"I'm sure there might be something else we can try," I said, trying hard to keep positive.

"Yeah, right." Rashida threw her head back on the seat behind her. "Our only hope now is finding Alice Grey."

I hadn't thought about my mother in such a long time. Alice Grey. I remembered when I'd first found out her maiden name. It was written on her ID badge from Neuro-Corp... Wait... It suddenly hit me. "Rashida!"

Rashida looked up, confused. "What?"

"Of course..." I mumbled as the memories rushed back to me. "Of course!" I turned the boat around, and Rashida jumped to her feet.

"What's going on?"

I glanced at her with a pleased smile. "I know how to find my mother."

CHAPTER 5

IT WAS WAY past midnight when we pulled up to my old apartment. There were still caution tapes fencing the property in, the walls and windows were charcoaled black and the burnt smell somehow still lingered in the air. Unless that was just my paranoia kicking in.

"Your mother is in there?" Rashida asked, not bothering to hide her skepticism.

"Of course not. Now keep your voice down." I crossed over the caution tapes and entered the garage. My heart squeezed when I pointed the flashlight toward my brother's tattoo station—what was left of it.

I forced myself to look away, suppressing the tears that came with all the memories.

"Then what the heck are we doing here?" Rashida whispered in a frustrated tone. "What's up there?"

I sucked in a breath, trying to control the whirlwind of emotions that came from knowing Ethan had also died there.

"Mia, talk to me."

"My mother's memory disc," I said, turning to look at her. "That's what's up there."

Rashida's eyes widened in disbelief. "I'm sorry," she chuckled. "I think the military training implant is really messing with my mind because I just heard you say that…" her expression turned suddenly serious, "you've had Alice Grey's memory this whole time."

"I didn't know that's what it was. Now, come on." I hurried up the stairs, and Rashida followed. We entered the loft careful but urgent, then rushed to the bedroom.

I scanned around for my computer and found it under a pile of things that were so burnt I couldn't even recognize it. I bit down on the flashlight and pulled my computer tower from underneath the rubble. "I need to get this open," I said, looking around. "I need something sharp."

Rashida pulled out a pocket knife. "Will this work?"

"You had a knife this whole time?" I asked, baffled. "Why did you give me a hairpin before?"

"That's what you asked for—"

The wooden floor squeaked in the living room, and we both turned toward the door. "What was that?" I whispered, fear creeping into my voice.

"I don't know," Rashida whispered back, bringing a hand to the back of her belt. Was she carrying a gun? "I'll go check it out. You, just hurry up and get that thing opened so we can get out of here."

Rashida took careful steps as she walked out of the room. The floor squeaked under her lightweight. I took a deep breath to steady my shaky hands then started to unscrew each corner, one by one.

Pots and pans clashed to the floor in the kitchen and Rashida ripped out a painful grunt. "We got company," she sang, unfazed. Then a screeching sound of glass breaking echoed off the walls. "Mia, hurry up!"

I turned to the tower and shoved the tip of the knife into the CD-ROM. It cracked under the pressure, but it still didn't open. There was a blatant kick on my bedroom door, and a tall field agent barged in.

"There you are."

I staggered to my feet, dropping the flashlight. The agent kicked the knife from my hand with a smile on his face. He grabbed me by my jacket and threw me across the room like I weighed no more than a pillow. My back banged against the wall and I fell to the floor.

The field agent was crouching down to reach for the tower, and I charged in his direction. He swerved out of the way and used my own momentum to slice my skin and push me against my dresser. My arm burned and when I touched it, it was wet. I looked at my shaking hand, and it was full of blood, the iron smell hitting me in the face and making me lightheaded.

He grabbed my jacket again and pinned me to the floor. "What's in the computer?" he hissed. "And don't lie." I felt the sharp tip of the pocket knife digging into my cheek. "You have three seconds to answer or else—"

A quick snapping sound echoed in the darkroom, and the man's body fell on top of me. I looked up only to find Rashida's small hands around his neck. Oh, God...she snapped it.

She pushed him off me like she was disposing of trash, then let out a tired breath. "Can we go, now?"

* * *

A FEW DAYS later while back at the island, I went to find Dale. I had tried cleaning the cut on my arm as best I could, but it was getting infected.

I entered the medical room and spotted Rashida sitting next to Victor's bed. He was sleeping, and she had her hand resting next to his. I could tell by the look on her face that she wanted to touch him.

"Mia!" Rashida jumped up and moved away from the bed. "I know I'm not supposed to be in here. I just wanted to know how he was doing. Please, don't tell Sophia."

"I won't," I assured her. "But you really can't be in here. We don't have any control over..." I pointed to our heads. "You know, the whole dormant effect thing."

She nodded. "Just please tell him I'm sorry when he wakes up."

"I will."

As soon as Rashida walked out, Victor opened his eyes and looked at me.

"You're awake?"

"Yep." He pushed himself to sit up, wincing as he strained his ribs. "The first time I pretended because, well, I was scared out of my mind. I mean, the girl almost killed me. But then she started crying and apologizing, and after that...I just started to enjoy her company."

"She's been sneaking in here?"

"I know, right!" He grinned. "Every time Sophia leaves, Bullet comes in and just sits with me."

"Bullet?"

"Oh, yeah. That's my new nickname for her," he said, proudly. "I mean, for a tiny little thing, she can do a lot of damage."

I laughed. "Something is seriously wrong with you."

"Yeah, well. We're all going nuts here."

"So, why do you pretend to be sleeping?" I asked, sitting on the chair Rashida had been. "Wouldn't your so-called relationship with her improve if you were awake?"

He lowered his head, his expression genuinely sad. "I'm afraid if she gets to apologize in person then she might stop coming."

"You really like her, huh?"

"It started as a joke." He shrugged. "I was bored, and the only entertainment I was getting in this place was annoying her. But it feels different now. I don't know how to describe it, but the few minutes that she spends sitting with me are the best minutes of my day."

"Good luck telling your sister that." I laughed, pulling off his blanket. "How's your leg?"

"Still kicking."

We heard a knock on the door and Dale peeked inside. "I heard you were looking for me?"

"Yeah…" I stood and unwrapped the bloody cloth around my arm. "What can I do about this?"

Dale came closer to examine it, and Victor leaned forward to look at it, too.

"What happened, M's?"

"Field agent cut me with a knife," I said, wincing at

Dale's touch. "If it weren't for Rashida and the military training, this cut would be the least of my worries."

Victor smiled. "Isn't she sexy?"

"I could stitch this up if you want me to," Dale said. "But I might have something better. My wife loves plants, and she got me experimenting with a few different herbal remedies. I think it can work."

"Okay, let's try that."

"It is experimental, though."

I shrugged. "I've already been a subject to a much worse experiment, doctor."

Dale chuckled. "Okay then, have a seat while I get it ready." He started toward the sink and picked up a plastic bowl. He mixed a few different things then after scooping a handful of cream, he pulled the metal tray to where I was and applied it to my wound.

"What is it?" I asked, watching.

"It's called shield tulsi," he said, lifting it so I can see. "It's a mixture of aloe, blagleek, parsnip, and adronna. They're plants, but you can find them in cream form over the counter. You mix it together, and it helps to disinfect the wound, speeding up the healing process. It works with practically anything. Burns, especially."

"Who got burned?" I asked.

"My wife, cooking the other day."

"Oh, I'm sorry. I had no idea."

"She's okay," he said, applying the last of the cream. "She's a tough cookie that woman. Alright, all done."

"Impressive, doc." Victor chimed in. "Can you put some of that on my leg so I can get out of this bed."

"Unfortunately, it doesn't heal bones," Dale said, going

to the sink and washing his hands. "But I will bring your some crutches."

Suddenly, a loud ping echoed in the room, and Dale stiffened. He cleared his throat nervously, then glanced at Victor.

"Are you serious?" I turned to Victor who held the most perfect poker face. "You've been using your cell phone?"

"What? Of course not." He pushed his back into his pillow like he was trying to find a comfortable position. "I heard the rule. I know we're not allowed to have cell phones."

"Oh, yeah?" I reached under his pillow, but he held it down, trapping my hand so I couldn't reach any further. "I can feel it, Victor!"

"All right, fine!" He let go, and I pulled out his cell phone. "But it's not connected. I swear. I downloaded a few games when we first got here but then I took the sim card out. I swear, M's! There's no way my dad could track it."

I glanced over my shoulder, looking for Dale but he'd left the room.

I looked back at Victor. "You really removed the sim card?"

"Yes."

I tossed the phone onto his lap, and he smiled, excited. "Thanks, M's!"

"We should go out there," I said, getting into position to help him up. "Benji should have bypassed the encryption of the disk by now."

* * *

IN THE CONFERENCE ROOM, Hugh sat next to Sophia, kissing her hand every five minutes. Her cheeks glowed with every kiss, and she blushed like a newlywed. It was cute. Victor sat next to me, with his injured leg propped on a chair in front of him. Rashida recoiled to the corner with Benji, her eyes discreetly flashing toward Victor. Dale sat in the back of the room with his wife.

"Got it," Archer finally said, inserting the disk into the computer and connecting the cable to the projector. "Turns out there was a CD with Alice's memory disc. It was encrypted, but Benji was able to hack it."

"What was it?" Hugh asked.

"A video."

"About?" Sophia asked, impatiently. "Will it help us out of this hell hole?"

"We haven't watched it, yet." Archer turned toward Benji and gave him a slight nod. The projector then turned on, and the video started loading. Archer moved out of the way and leaned against the side wall.

I sucked in a nervous breath. I couldn't believe I was finally going to see my mother and know what she looked like. Hugh glanced over at me with an encouraging smile. I reached for Victor's hand and squeezed it.

"Archer, my love..." When my mother's face appeared on the wall, I squeezed Victor's hand even tighter. She was so beautiful. Even with bags under her eyes, she looked absolutely stunning. But she also looked familiar, like I'd seen her before. Her eyes were green like mine, but she had brown hair like Shawn, though hers was longer and it cascaded over her shoulders.

"If you're watching this video," she continued, "then you

found the key I hid in our favorite book." She smiled. "That was the book you pretended I'd left it behind so you had an excuse to come talk to me, remember?"

"Grey, hurry up." A man's voice rushed her from behind the camera, and we all glanced at one another with the same question plastered on our faces. Who was that?

When I looked at Archer, he had sunk to the floor and was grabbing his head, his face twisting in excruciating pain. The same pain he felt the day he saw the journal— Oh. My. God.

Archer was having a surge.

My mother's voice snapped me back to the video. "I finally made the breakthrough, but now they want it for something else. I can't let them have it. I meant for this research to help people, not control them. I know this all sounds crazy, but I don't have time to go into detail right now. I'm still at the lab, and we're running out of time. I already deleted all of my research from their system, but that won't be enough," her voice cracked a little, "I have to delete... everything."

"Grey, we have to go." The voice interrupted again, and she nodded.

"I asked Collins Sr. to erase my memory," she went on, looking into the camera. "Trust me, this is the only way. My love, if all goes according to plan, I will see you soon, sweetheart." She forced a smile despite all the anxiety she was clearly feeling. "You'll know where to find me—"

"Darn it, Grey, you're gonna get us killed!" Collins' voice urged again, and tears started to fill my mother's eyes.

"If things don't go according to plan," she choked up as

she continued. "Please tell Shawny and Mia that I love them with all my heart. And that if I had any other choice, I would take it. Archer, I love you. I love you with all my heart." She leaned forward and turned off the camera, and just like that, everything went black.

I looked for Archer—he was still on the floor grabbing his head. Dale crouched at his side and laid a hand on his shoulder. There wasn't anything else he could do.

"So, that was your mom?" Rashida broke the silence, looking at me from across the room.

"No," Sophia cut in, even though she knew the question wasn't meant for her. "That was my mom."

CHAPTER 6

*T*HE PROJECTOR had been off for a long time, but still, no one could get their eyes off the blank wall.

"I don't get it," Victor finally broke the silence. "So, Alice Grey and Helen Hemsworth are the same person?"

"Yes." My voice was barely above a whisper. "It seems so."

Victor shook his head. "But how?"

"Dad must've taken Alice after she erased her own memory," Sophia suggested, her eyes widened in shock. "He could've made up any lie to get her to go with him."

"So..." Victor turned to face me, his hand still clutching mine. "Does this mean you're my sister, too?"

I could barely manage a nod.

"Did you know about this?" Sophia's turned to Hugh, her face was so pale, it looked like she was going to pass out at any moment.

"No." Hugh upped his hands, defensively. "I knew that

my father had worked with Alice, but that's it. I had no idea about any of this. I swear."

Sophia looked appalled. "What did your father do to her?" She pulled her hands away from Hugh. "Is that what caused her Alzheimer's?"

"Your mother doesn't have Alzheimer's," Rashida cut in, sinking into her chair. "Your father put her through the Catalyst so many times, it fried her brain."

Sophia gasped and brought a clutching hand to her heart. "No." She reached to grab the table. "He wouldn't have... He couldn't have." Sophia's voice started to shudder. Hugh reached for her hand.

"Every time he suspected she remembered something," Rashida continued, "he brought her in for a procedure. If we hadn't seen it for ourselves—"

"What do you mean, we?" Sophia pressed.

Hugh shot Rashida a frightened glance, and she pressed her lips together.

Sophia turned slowly to Hugh. "You knew?"

Hugh opened his mouth to deny but he couldn't. Sophia ripped her hand away from him and paced around like she wanted to punch something. "Oh, my God! You knew! You knew she didn't have Alzheimer's!"

"I'm sorry—"

"How long?" she hissed. "How long have you known?"

Hugh's eyes began to water as if he knew his words were going to cause a world of pain and there was nothing he could do to stop it. "Ever since I started working for your father."

Sophia gasped.

Hugh threw himself back into his chair and buried his

face in his hands. He knew Sophia couldn't bear to look at him and he couldn't blame her.

"Your father threatened him." Rashida came to his defense. "I was there. I heard him. Your father said that if you ever found out, he would put you through the Catalyst, too. Hugh was just trying to protect you."

"You..." Sophia glared at Rashida. "Don't talk to me, ever. And you..." Sophia looked at Hugh in disgust. She opened her mouth to speak, but her anger sapped her words.

Hugh looked up with tears in his eyes. "I am so sorry—"

"Don't." Sophia looked away as if just the sight of him burned her eyes. She stiffened her jaw, trying to keep it together, trying not to fall apart, but her hands started to shake. "We're done." She stormed out the door and finally gave in to her sobs in the hallway.

Hugh tried to follow, but Victor jumped up and put a hand on his chest. "I got it." Victor turned around and skipped after his sister, holding on to the walls for support.

Hugh took a seat next to me, his expression drained. "I swear I had no idea that Helen was Alice Grey. My dad never told me."

"I believe you." I gave him a reassuring nod, and he forced his lips together, trying to keep his emotions at bay.

"I was just trying to protect her." He buried his face into his hands. "She's never gonna forgive me."

"Word of advice..." I put a hand on his trembling shoulder. "Stop keeping secrets."

* * *

It was four in the morning, and I couldn't sleep. I entered the break room, and Archer was sitting on a chair, holding a cup of tea.

"Couldn't sleep either?" I asked, sitting across from him.

He nodded but didn't say anything else.

"It makes sense that Hemsworth put you through the Catalyst," I said, finally addressing what I had seen in the conference room. "He needed to make sure you wouldn't get in his way of him taking Mom."

"That explains a lot." Archer breathed, still in disbelief. "When I woke up at that hospital, I had no idea who I even was. I was told I was a single father of two kids and that my wife had left me. How in the world was I supposed to handle a toddler and a baby on my own?" He ran his fingers through his gray hair as he stared across the room. "I had no idea what to do. All I knew was that every time I looked at Shawn, I got these strange flashes of Alice and my head felt like it was going to explode."

"You were having surges."

He shook his head. "I had no idea what they were. It was just excruciating, and I wanted it to stop. So... I started drinking."

"You said Shawn reminded you of Mom..." I fidgeted with my fingers. Talking to Archer about Shawn still wasn't easy. "Is that why you would beat him?"

"Beat him?" Archer looked at me as if I'd slapped him. "You saw me beat him?" He asked, concerned that perhaps he may not have been remembering things correctly. "You saw me physically hit him?"

"I used to hear him crying and yelling and glass breaking all over the house."

"Oh, that..." Archer waved it off. "He would hide my bottles then get upset when I would find them. He would start crying, ask me to stop, then break my bottles. I might've yelled at him, but I never laid a hand on him, Mia."

The more I thought about it, the more I realized that Shawn never actually said he'd been physically abused by Archer. I had just always assumed.

Benji cleared his throat. "I'm sorry to interrupt, but... I was able to unlock the floppy disk. Alice's memories are ready to be inserted."

"Inserted?" I looked at Archer, confused. "Shouldn't we wait and give it back to her?"

"We can insert the same memories more than once," Benji explained. "It's just a matter of choosing the proper setting in the computer. Anyway, just let me know whenever you're ready."

"Me?" I chuckled. "I don't think so."

Rashida walked in and looked from Benji to me. "Ready?"

Benji shrugged, his expression at a loss. "She doesn't want it."

"What?" Rashida shot a disbelieving glance at me. "Okay, somebody's gotta have it. Otherwise, we're back to square one."

"Why not you?" I asked Rashida.

"Oh, no." Rashida's face twisted as if she had eaten a sour candy. "She gave birth to Victor. I can't be feeling any motherly instinct toward him. It'll feel wrong in so many levels."

Feel wrong? Was she starting to like him?

"Why don't you want it?" Rashida asked me, puzzled.

I took a deep breath and seriously considered it. "Once the Order finds out we have my mother's memories, they will automatically assume I have it. That could work to our advantage." Also, my mother slept with my father, and I really didn't want those images in my head, but I kept that to myself.

Rashida nodded. "I hadn't thought about that."

I glanced at Archer who still hung his head low. "Archer should have it," I said.

Archer shot up a glance at me, shocked. "What? Me? You're sure?"

"She left it for you." I shrugged. "It's only fair that you take it." I looked around the room, and my expression was suddenly serious. "But no one can know about this. Only us four, in this room. Is that clear?"

They all nodded.

"Good." I stood and headed toward the door. "Let me know when it's done."

* * *

THE SUN WAS GRADUALLY SETTING when I sat on the edge of the cliff with my legs hanging loose. I took in the beautiful sight hoping to give my mind a break from the whirlwind of thoughts spinning in my head.

Mom didn't leave us, she was kidnapped. I wish Shawn knew that. Maybe he wouldn't have hated her so much if he knew she didn't mean to leave. If he knew she was just trying to protect us.

"Hey," Sophia's voice came from behind me. "I knew I

would find you here." She took a seat next to me and let out a breath of disbelief. "I still can't believe we're sisters." It looked like she was about to pull out her own hair but then her eyes met mine, and she sighed. "I'm so sorry my father ruined your family."

I shrugged. "It's bittersweet, I guess."

"What do you mean?"

"As much as I hate your father for what he did. If he hadn't done it, you and Victor wouldn't exist, and I honestly don't know what I would do without you both."

She smiled then nudged me with her shoulder. "Agreed."

I nudged her back, and for a little while, we laughed together. But then, she stopped. "I want to go get Mom. Will you help me?"

"I want that too, but..." I looked around the deserted island. "We can't just bring her here. We don't even know how to treat her."

She groaned in frustration as she pushed herself to her feet. "I can't just leave her with him. All of those treatments he took her to... I should've known something was wrong."

"Don't beat yourself up." I stood with her. "Guilt isn't gonna help. There was no way you could've known what he was doing."

"I just can't believe how many times he's done it. I mean, he literally fried her brain." She choked back her tears. "If he could do that to his own wife, imagine what he's doing to other people."

I put a hand on her shoulder, and she looked out to the ocean. "We will shut them down. Even if it's the last thing I do. I promise."

Sophia shook her head. "I can't leave her for that long."

"No one is leaving her," I assured. "All I'm saying is that right now we need to focus on bringing down the Order. Then we can leave this island and take her somewhere safe, as far away from your dad as possible."

She buried her face in her hands and started to cry. "I can't believe Hugh knew, Mia. All these years, he knew. How could I ever forgive him?" she cried, sitting back down. "How could I ever trust him, again?"

"One step at a time," I said. "That's all we can do right now."

"Sista, sistas!" Victor sang like it was a theme song or something. I gave Sophia a quizzical look, but she just rolled her eyes and wiped her face.

"Check this out!" Victor held up a paintball gun with the widest grin on his face. "Pretty awesome, huh?"

"So, it's a paintball gun. Big deal." Sophia crossed her arms, unimpressed.

Victor raised a finger with an eager wait-for-it expression. "Not quite," he said, clicking it open and rolling a smooth metal ball into his hand. "See? Instead of shooting paintballs, I changed it so that it shoots... Wait for it... Taser bullets!" His mouth dropped open for effect, but Sophia still looked unimpressed. "Oh, come on!" He looked at me, hoping for a different reaction.

"Cool."

"Cool?" he echoed, disappointed. "Come on, guys! A little support here. We're all family."

"Fine." Sophia took one of the bullets and examined it. It was the size of a jawbreaker. "What does it do?"

Victor took another ball from inside the gun and held it

up with renewed enthusiasm. "You shoot one of these, and it shocks them like a taser—incapacitating them for a few minutes. You shoot two, it paralyzes them for a few hours. You shoot three..." he paused. "They're dead."

"Wow," I breathed, taking the ball from Sophia. "That's pretty genius."

Victor gave a smug face. "I'm sorry, did you expect anything less?"

I slapped his arm. "So, how does it work?"

"Pretty easy." He inserted both bullets back into the gun and clicked it closed. "See? It's all set."

"Hey, Victor." Hugh approached, keeping his head down. "Rashida is looking for you. She has a question about those taser bullets."

Sophia clenched her jaw, and I wasn't sure if it was Hugh's presence alone that annoyed her, or if it was the fact that he came bearing a message from Rashida of all people.

When Hugh turned around to walk away, Sophia snatched the gun from Victor's hand and pointed at Hugh's back. She pulled the trigger once and while in mid-air, spikes came out of the metal ball. When it pierced into Hugh's back, it threw his body into a violent convulsion then dropped him to the ground.

"Nice job, little brother." Sophia smiled, giving Victor back his gun. "It works great."

I peeked into Archer's room. He was lying on his bed staring at the ceiling. I cleared my throat, and he snapped out of his trance. "Oh, hi."

"Hi." I walked in, leaving the door open behind me. "I brought you some tea. And the meds for your heart." My heart ached as I remembered the day Shawn told me he'd gotten tested. He also had the same heart condition.

"Thank you." Archer pushed himself to sit up, and I handed him the cup and the pill. "You didn't have to do that."

"How are you feeling?" I asked, sitting next to his bed.

"Still a little groggy," he said, leaning his head back on the wall. "The sedation is lingering a bit."

"How long is it supposed to last?"

"It depends." He took a sip of the tea. "They had to run the procedure twice."

"Why?"

"Once I got Alice's memory, I figured out that the Catalyst procedure should be done a lot slower. It was never intended to be rushed. That's the reason for the glitches. It's like a brain freeze. You have to drink it slowly, to give the body time to adapt to the shock."

"How does it feel?" I asked, curious. "Having Mom's memories, I mean."

"Everything is so clear," he said, baffled. "I remember everything now. Even though it's from her perspective and not mine, it doesn't seem to matter. It's still our life together." He paused and turned to look at me. "I can see how she felt when she held you in her arms for the first time." His eyes started welling up with tears. "She loved you so much..." his voice cracked, and he looked down at his tea.

I felt a slight tug in my heart at the confirmation that my mother did love me.

"Anyway..." Archer shook his head. "There was so much more in those missing pages, you wouldn't believe."

"Like what?"

"She came up with a feature for the Catalyst called mind-lock. It blocks the Catalyst machine from removing the memory. It's as if it creates a shield."

I perked up with sudden interest. "So, the memories can't ever be removed?"

"Well…not quite," he said. "The mind-lock resets every twenty-four hours. You have to allow your mind to rest within that window; otherwise, it will deactivate."

"What if you just can't sleep?"

"Then you need to force your mind to turn off some other way. Blacking-out would work just the same."

"Why didn't she use it on herself?" I asked.

"She didn't have time to test it."

"Is your mind locked now?"

He nodded. "We cannot let the Order get their hands on what Alice knows."

"What else did she know?" I asked, Archer looked toward the opened door.

"Shut the door," he said.

I did as he asked then came back to sit next to his bed. "What is it?"

"Her last breakthrough was mind control."

"Mind control?"

He nodded. "Your mother did this experiment where she was able to brainwash a subject just by making them watch a video on a screen."

"How is that possible?"

Archer pushed himself to his feet and went to stand next to a TV in the far corner of the room. "She converted the pixels in the TV to flash just like the lights in the Catalyst machine, so whatever video is playing is implanting into the person's mind as absolute truth."

"Oh, wow."

"Exactly." Archer sat at the edge of his bed. "Now it makes sense why she panicked and put herself through the Catalyst. Who knows what the Order could do with this kind of power."

"What were they planning?" I asked.

Archer shook his head. "They never told her, but she was smart enough to know it wasn't good." Archer winced and brought a hand to his head. "Sorry, I'm still adjusting."

"Well, I'll leave you to rest some more," I said, standing. "Oh, and don't tell anyone else what you just told me."

"Why are you all of a sudden worried about that?" Archer asked. "Is there someone here we shouldn't trust?"

"It's not that I don't trust them," I clarified. "I think we all want the same goal—to bring down the Order. But we're not all on the same agenda, and I don't want you caught in the middle."

"Sounds like..." Archer didn't seem sure how to phrase it, "you're looking out for me."

"That sounds about right."

* * *

ON MY WAY out of Archer's room, I crashed onto Dale's wife.

"Oh, hey. Sorry..." I motioned my closed fist over my chest, trying to sign my apology, but she stopped me and grabbed my arm. She began to sign something I couldn't understand. She was sweating and kept looking over her shoulder. I focused on her hands. Somebody was walking under a roof? What did that mean?

"I'm sorry, I don't understand." I glanced over my shoulder. "We should get Dale—"

She huffed in frustration, but I wasn't sure what else I could do. She let out a defeated sigh and disappeared into the conference room. At this, Victor came whistling down the hall.

"Hey. Can you help me understand Anne? She's trying to tell me something—Wait, where's Sophia? Wasn't she with you?"

"Huh? Oh, you mean my sister? Uh…" He looked down, and I could tell he was purposely avoiding my eyes.

I made my way toward him, and he started to sweat. "Victor?"

"Yeah?"

Why was he stalling? "Where's Sophia?"

"She's, uh…You know what? I'm not actually sure. I just got out of the shower."

"Is that right?" I stepped in front of him and crossed my arms. "Why isn't your hair wet?"

"My hair?" He touched his dry hair and froze. "Oh, I didn't feel like washing it today. They say it's not good to shampoo too much—"

I grabbed Victor by the collar of his shirt and pinned him against the wall. "Where is she, Victor?"

He opened his mouth to keep lying, but I banged him against the wall, again.

"Fine! She went to get Mom!"

"What?" My eyes widened. "When?"

"I just came back from dropping her off at the marina,"

he confessed, his shoulders sagging. "I'm sorry M's, but she's right. We can't just leave Mom with that monster."

"God, Victor!" I let go of his shirt, fighting back the urge to slap him. "She's not going to find Mom."

Victor stood there, speechless. "What do you mean?"

I rubbed my hands on my face. "She's going to confront your dad."

Victor sunk to the floor. "She lied to me?"

"What's going on?" Hugh came out of the conference room, shooting a concerned look toward me.

"Sophia is gone," I said bluntly, like ripping off a band-aid.

"What do you mean...gone?" Hugh's blood drained from his face.

"I thought she was going to get Mom," Victor said, deflated. "Oh, man. They're gonna get her, aren't they? They probably already did..." he trailed off, burying his face in his hands.

Hugh turned to me, almost in the verge of panic. "Can we make it in time to stop her?"

"Guys?" Rashida peeped out of the conference room. "Dale is looking for his car keys. Has anyone seen it?"

I looked at Hugh. "Does that answer your question?"

Victor sunk lower to the floor.

"What's going on?" Rashida stepped out to the hallway, noticing the tension. "Hugh?"

"Sophia's gone."

"What?" Rashida looked at me for confirmation, and I nodded. "Where in the world would she go?"

"To get her mother—Wait! Victor, do you still have your

phone on you?" Hugh asked, and Victor nodded. "Can you track her location?"

"Are you out of your mind?" Rashida turned Hugh around and made him look her in the eyes. "We turn that thing on, and Hemsworth is going to track us!"

"That's a risk I'm willing to take," Hugh said in a firm tone. "I'm sorry, but she won't make it out there on her own."

"She chose to go."

"I don't care." Hugh turned to Victor, unyielding. "Where is your phone?" He helped Victor up, and they both sprang down the hall.

Rashida watched both of them in disbelief, then turned to look at me. "We're gonna get caught."

"We would have to leave the island, either way," I said. "Once they take Sophia's memory, they'll find out where we'd been hiding."

"So, now what?"

"Now," I said, bracing myself, "you give us that military training."

CHAPTER 7

I STOOD MOTIONLESS under the shower head. The heat of the water against my skin did nothing to wash away the tension I felt inside. I couldn't help but wonder if Sophia had already been caught. Had they taken her memory? How much longer did we have until they came for us?

After I finished getting dressed, I heard the sound of one of the shower curtains move.

"Hello?" I turned around still drying my damped hair with the towel. "Victor, if you're hiding in here…" I clenched my jaw as I made my way further into the locker room, looking into each stall at a time. "Stop right now, it's not funny."

As I got to the last stall, I noticed the shower curtain swaying. I reached to grab it, but before I could touch it, a field agent jumped out and lunged in my direction. I screamed, but he immediately reached to cover my mouth, muffling the sound. He pushed me back into another stall and pinned me against the wall, sealing his hand over my mouth even tighter. He pulled a handkerchief from his pocket, and as he brought it close to my face, I could sense the strong smell of the chemical.

I jerked my knee up into his groin, and as soon as his hand dropped from my face, I screamed as loud as I could. I pushed him as I ran past, but in his quick reflex, he slapped my foot and threw me off balance. I stumbled to the wet floor, and a second later his chest was pressed against my back. He was heavy on top of me. His hand sealed my mouth a second time, and so did his handkerchief. I held my breath trying not to inhale the fume, but the chemical was so strong; it stung my eyes.

Stop panicking. Focus. You're not defenseless anymore.

I closed my eyes and thought of the military training. The knowledge gave me confidence, and my body began to relax. It wasn't about strength, it was about control, technique, and pressure points.

I grabbed his forearm and jerked it to the side, hitting the funny bone of his elbow on the stall. He staggered off me as his arm dropped dead. I flipped around and stomped his knee cap. He ripped out a grunt as his body collapsed to the floor in excruciating pain. I saddled atop of him and grabbed the front of his throat. He grabbed my arm, his eyes widened in panic. I pushed his windpipe with my thumb, making it hard for him to breathe as I cut off his oxygen. Within seconds, his eyes rolled back, and he blacked out.

I exhaled the tension and fell next to his limp body with the muscles of my arms throbbing. Hugh stood by the door with his mouth agape.

"Oh, hey. Bad news," I said, still trying to catch my breath. "They're here."

I peeked through a thick thorn bush and looked down at the beach. The night air was cold, and the thin fabric of the scrubs did little to keep me warm. I scooted closer to Victor, who was lying on the grass next to me.

"There they are," Victor said, and I lifted up my head to see. A large black yacht was docked away from the rocks while a motorized float boat brought the field agents to shore. They swarmed onto the island like ants—but unlike before, we were finally ready for them.

We watched as they moved up the hill like a S.W.A.T. team. Although they were quiet, the moon was bright enough where we could watch their every move.

"Ready?" I whispered to Victor, and he nodded. We crawled toward the rocky cliff. Victor winced as he put pressure on his ribs which were still not fully healed. We looked over the edge. Victor stared down into the water with a slight hint of fear in his eyes. That same cliff almost killed him. He took a deep breath, and I reached for his hand.

"It's gonna work," I assured him, giving his hand a light squeeze. I glanced at my watch, it was exactly midnight. I looked back at him. "Ready?"

He nodded.

I stood quickly and jumped off the cliff. I tucked my arms close to my body and pointed my toes as I hit the dark water. The freezing temperature engulfed me. I hurried back to the surface and looked up. I pressed the light on my watch as a signal to Victor, and he jumped, splashing down a few feet away from me. He came up coughing, and I let out a sigh of relief. I swam toward him and covered his mouth.

"Stop making noise," I whispered. "It's best if they don't see us coming,"

"Sorry," Victor whispered back.

We started swimming toward the NeuroCorp mega yacht, all the while trying to avoid splashing around. Victor kept huffing and I could tell that swimming was putting a lot of strain on his injured leg, as well as his ribs.

"We're almost there," I encouraged. "Grab on to me if you need to."

"I'm fine."

The motorized float was leaving the yacht with its last set of agents, and I pushed Victor's head down into the water, going down with him. The boat passed over us. I held Victor down until the engine was as far away as possible, then finally tugged on his scrubs. We both swam up to the surface, gasping for air.

We swam to the ladder that hung down from the side of the boat, and the smell of smoke came from up top. I tugged on the rope to make sure it was firm.

"Hey, M's..." Victor put his shivering hand on my shoulder. "I don't know how many agents you're going up against here but can you like, hurry up and knock them out? I'm freezing."

"Anything else, your highness?" I whispered.

"Some hot cocoa would be nice."

I rolled my eyes then firmed my grip on the ladder. I climbed as quietly as I could, trying to keep my body from shivering from the piercing chill of the wind. The sound of my wet sneakers hitting the solid deck caught the attention of the two agents who were sitting out back, playing cards. They jumped to their feet, knocking over the flimsy wood table between them. They spat their cigarettes out and darted toward me.

The first agent drew his weapon, but I kicked it from his hand, and it slid off the boat. My next blow sent him flying over the edge of the yacht. His startled cry was cut short as he hit the water with a loud splash.

"I'm alright!" Victor yelled from the ladder as he started climbing up to the deck.

The second agent lunged forward and wrestled me to the slippery floor. I reached for one of the lit cigarettes and pressed it to his cheek. He yelled, bringing his hands to his face. I punched him in the stomach then kneed him on the lungs. As he gasped for air, I pushed him off of me and shifted my entire body weight onto him. His eyes rolled back before I even realized my hands were around his neck.

I pulled away.

The man's limp body slumped to the floor. He was unconscious but still breathing. I dropped next to him, my hand shaking. Despite still being cold, the adrenaline of almost killing a man made my heart pound. I had to find a way to control the military training, rather than letting it control me.

A hand grabbed my wet hair, and I let out a screeching yelp. I was thrown across the deck and fell with my back to the floor. Another field agent charged in my direction. I grabbed the small table by its leg and swung toward him.

The wood broke against his arm, and he staggered backward. As he lost his balance, I kicked him on the chest, throwing him off the boat.

"M's!" Victor yelled, and I ran to the ladder. The agent had grabbed hold of Victor's injured leg and was hanging on to him.

"Victor, hold on!"

Victor screamed, wrapping his arms around the ladder, trying hard not to let go. I ran back to the agent that was still passed out, confiscated his weapon, then rushed back to Victor. I aimed the gun, trying to focus on the agent but he kept using Victor as a shield.

The agent punched Victor in his ribs, and Victor let out the most excruciating cry I'd ever heard. The sound propelled me forward, and I jumped off the yacht, all the while aiming the gun at the agent's back on my way down. I pulled the trigger and shot him on the shoulder. We both splashed into the dark water. Though I couldn't see anything, I could hear the agent's painful cry underwater as well as his panicked strokes as he swam back to the surface. I snuck up behind him and pulled the trigger a second time—on his other shoulder. He screamed, and I pushed his head down into the water.

I shoved the gun behind my pants and reached to grab the ladder. "Victor!" I called out, climbing toward him. When I reached him, he was crying. The sound nearly shattered my heart.

"C'mon..." I hooked his arm around my neck and pulled him up. "I know it hurts, but I'm gonna need you to push."

Victor sucked back his tears and nodded. It took way too long to get back to the top, but we finally made it.

The agent on the floor moaned as he slowly regained consciousness. He crawled to his knees and came to his full senses when he saw me holding a firearm in his direction.

"Go help your friend before he drowns," I said, still holding on to Victor.

The agent gave a slight nod as he got to his feet. He scrambled over the edge of the yacht and jumped into the ocean. I lowered the weapon then eased Victor down to the floor.

"Remind me," Victor said, grimacing in pain, "to never mess with you on a bad day."

I smiled. Hearing him joke again lifted all the worry that was weighing down my heart. "I'll be right back," I told him.

He nodded, closing his eyes and leaning his back against the wall.

"Hey!" I slapped his face a couple times, and he opened his eyes. "I need you to stay awake. Here..." I handed him the gun. "Keep a lookout. Shoot at any agent that comes up this ladder. Got it?"

"Ay ay, captain."

I darted off to the engine room, wiping my wet, matted hair away from my face. I ripped the wires from the GPS then flipped the switch for the spotlight above the yacht. I turned it on and off twice then ran to the side of the boat and stared up at the cliff, waiting.

"C'mon, C'mon…" I whispered softly. "Hurry up."

Hugh and Rashida appeared in the distance running

side by side toward the edge of the cliff. They jumped, and I held my breath.

Seconds later, an explosion rocked the island. The blast sent the battalion of agents to the ground. Plumes of fire and smoke rose from the laboratory into the dark sky. Hugh and Rashida emerged from the water unharmed.

"Hey, M's..." Victor mumbled. "Can we not tell Bullet about me crying like a baby? It'll be such a turn-off."

I chuckled. "Shut up and rest."

"I'm just sayin'."

I rushed to the ladder to help Rashida up. "Where's Hugh?" I asked.

She turned around, and we both looked down. Hugh was struggling with an agent on top of the float boat.

"Over here!" A young man's voice called out in the distance, it came from the other side of the yacht. I ran across the deck and looked down. Benji waved with a relieved smile. Archer stood next to him, along with Dale and his wife. They were all in Dale's fishing boat.

Rashida crossed the deck with the ladder in her hand, and we threw it down to them. They each climbed up as fast as they could, but Benji and Archer were carrying large backpacks which slowed them down.

"Hurry up!" Hugh yelled, coming around steering the motor of the float boat. "The agents are starting to swim toward us. We gotta go."

Rashida helped Benji up, and they immediately darted toward the engine room. I pulled up Archer, then he helped with Dale and his wife.

"Hugh, hurry!" I yelled, watching as the calm waters

turned turbulent from the tons of agents that were swimming toward the yacht.

"We have to pull it up," Dale said with an instant panic. But when he reached for the ladder, I held his hand.

"Not yet," I said.

"They're going to climb—"

"I got this. Go check on Victor." I leaned over the railing. "Hugh, hurry!"

Hugh tied the float onto the fishing boat then pushed the lever to get Dale's boat moving out to the open sea. As the boat began gaining momentum, Hugh ran to the back. He jumped off just as the boat started to speed. He grabbed onto the ladder with five agents at his tale.

"Now!" he yelled.

Archer threw off his backpack and reached for the ladder. We pulled it up as fast as we could, but it was too heavy. If felt like we were pulling the weight of two people. One of the agents must've grabbed hold of the end of the ladder. The ladder started to move and tug—they must've been struggling. Archer's hand slipped, and the heavyweight yanked my body forward. I hung over the railing, refusing to let go. Hugh kicked the agent in the face, and he dropped from halfway up, falling on top of another agent.

Archer grabbed the ladder again, and we kept pulling until Hugh finally collapsed into the yacht. We all dropped to the wooden floor, gasping for air. When the yacht started to move, I turned to Hugh.

"Why did you blow up the lab?" I asked, out of breath.

Hugh opened his eyes and looked at me. "It was the fastest way to kill the phone signal. They'll know how to fix it, but by the time they do and get another boat here, we would have already gotten Sophia and the hard drive."

"Hey, guys!" Benji peeked his head out. "Come check out their control room. These computers are top of the line."

"And these gadgets," Rashida added, holding what looked like night vision goggles. "Sweet!"

CHAPTER 8

*T*HE NEUROCORP headquarters was located three hours northeast of Bunker Hill, in the middle of the forest. On top of that, we had to hike another hour up a mountain. If we hadn't been tracking Sophia's phone, we probably would never have found it. Even the map gave nothing more than latitude and longitude coordinates.

By the time we finally found the building, it was already four in the morning, which meant we had less than three hours to get in and out of there before sunrise. According to Rashida, there were fewer guards on post during the night and hardly any nurses, which increased our odds— though not by much. We were still outnumbered. Victor was too injured to come, and Archer's mind, at the moment, was too valuable to risk. Dale and his wife never got the military training, so they stayed behind. Benji stayed on the boat with his laptop guiding us through an earpiece, using satellite images of the compound.

That left only Hugh, Rashida, and me to do the bulk of

the work. At least we were well equipped—not only were we connected through an earpiece we found on the yacht, but we also had night-vision goggles and bulletproof vests that came with the field agent uniforms.

"The whole building is surrounded by a ten-foot chain link fence," Benji said through the earpiece. "Except the back of the building, but it's barely hanging off a steep hill."

"Where is Sophia?" Hugh asked, like that was the only thing that mattered.

"I can't tell the exact location. I can only see heat sensors from here," Benji explained. "But her phone is flashing on the east wing."

"Where is the vault?" I asked.

"Let me see…" Benji typed on his laptop. "Okay, got it. There should be a latch on the ground about ten feet north of where Rashida is. Pull it open. There should be a tunnel that will lead you to the underground floor of the building."

"How many guards?" Rashida asked.

"Three, maybe five."

Rashida hurried to the precise location, and after dusting off the leaves from the ground, she hooked her finger on the latch. Hugh helped her pull it open. I slipped on my night vision goggle and raised my taser gun, doing a perimeter check. Everything was quiet except the cicadas echoing in the night.

"Benji, where is Hemsworth's office?" I asked.

Benji typed on his keyboard. "Third floor. Looks like someone's there now."

"Alright, this is it," I whispered, turning to Hugh and Rashida. "We need to stick to the escape plan, no matter what happens. Hugh, you'll take Sophia the way we came and get to Dale's car as fast as you can. Rashida, as soon as you get the drive, you hurry out of there and flee to the opposite direction and do whatever you gotta do to get to the marina." I raised a finger of authority and looked at both of them in the eyes. "We do not wait for each other. We do not come back for one another. We run and meet back at the boat. Understood?"

They nodded.

"Good." I pointed to Rashida. "You go for the drive. Hugh and I will go through the back and try to lure the guards away from your end."

Rashida nodded then slipped on her night vision goggle as she carefully entered the tunnel, her taser gun positioned below her chin.

Hugh and I took off running through the woods, swerving through the trees. When we got to the fence, Hugh put an arm across my chest, stopping me.

"It's an electric fence," he warned.

We looked down and at the bottom of the steep hill was a violent river. We could see the foam in the moonlight, carrying tree branches of all shapes and sizes.

"We won't make it," he added, assessing our odds. "Even if we go down to the bottom and hike our way up, we'll waste too much time. We should go back to the tunnel."

"Maybe not." I picked up a large rock from the ground and shoved it in my pocket. "I have an idea. Follow me."

I climbed a tree all the way to the top, it was bare with no leaves—thankfully we were wearing black field agent uniforms. Hugh followed close behind. Once I found a sturdy branch, I laid flat on my stomach.

"Hold on," I whispered, and Hugh stopped. I swung my gun forward and aimed at the green light flashing on the camera at the corner of the building. I released one shot and the electricity of the taser bullet fried the camera instantly.

I threw the gun behind my back and tightened the strap. "Benji, can you cut the rest of the cameras?"

"I can try," he responded.

I pushed myself up and hopped onto the next tree. The branch cracked under my weight and Hugh caught my arm, wrapping his long fingers around it. "I got you."

"Guys, a little help here," Rashida whispered through the earpiece. "Still got three agents guarding the door."

Hugh pulled me back up, and I regained my footing on another branch. "Working on it," I said, hopping onto to the next tree; Hugh following close behind me. "Get ready, I'm about to distract them."

I stopped and turned toward the building, facing a large glass window. "Benji...how many guards on the second floor?" I asked in a hushed tone as I took the rock from my pocket.

"Five...for now."

I threw the rock at the second-floor window, and the glass shattered immediately upon impact. The alarm went off, echoing through the whole building. I ran for momentum then leaped in the air, diving through the broken window. I tucked and rolled as I hit the white tile floor. I swung my gun forward and shot at one guard, then another. Hugh was already behind me, shooting at the other three guards.

"Subtle," he teased over the siren.

"Got it," Rashida said from her end. "Thanks, guys."

"Mia! Hugh! Get out of there!" Benji warned. "Seven guards are on their way! No...eleven! Get in the room on your left. Hurry!"

We rushed to follow Benji's instructions. Hugh locked the door behind us. "There's no way out," Hugh told Benji.

"Through the vents," Benji said. "And keep your goggles on. I'm gonna try to turn off the lights."

The room was dark, and Hugh reached for something made out of metal that was on top of the counter. He dug into the vent cover and broke it open.

"You go first," he said, crouching underneath the vent and offering his hand as a step stool. "Come on."

I jumped into the vent and crawled as fast as I could. Still, Hugh kept pushing me to go faster.

"Mia...Hugh. The guards are all rushing to the second floor," Benji said. "You'll need to climb to the top. There should be an opening ten feet ahead from where you are."

I stopped under the opening and looked up. "I see it," I told Benji as I stood. I jumped up, supporting my hands and feet on opposite sides of the metal wall and pushed myself up. "How far up?" I asked, as my arms began to weaken.

"Two floors," Benji said. "Now, one floor and a half."

I stopped to catch my breath.

"Don't stop," Hugh rushed me. "You'll get tired faster. Just keep going."

I pushed harder. "How much further?" I asked Benji, but he didn't respond. "Benji? Rashida?"

"The reception is cutting off," Hugh said, his voice strained. "Just keep going, Mia."

I finally reached a horizontal vent and threw myself inside, making enough room for Hugh to jump into it, also. We collapsed out of breath. "Benji?" I called out, but still nothing.

I crawled further into the vent and stopped by an opening that led to another exam room. It was empty, and the lights were off, but as I peeked through the opening, I saw guards pacing on the hallway. I pushed my back against the metal wall, giving Hugh enough room to take a peek.

"What do we do now?" I asked, pushing the goggles up to the top of my head. The green light was giving me a headache.

Hugh pressed into his earpiece. "Benji, can you hear me?" he whispered, leaning his ear as close to the opening of the vent as possible. "Benji?"

"Hu—" Benji's voice kept cutting in and out. "I—hear—" Static muffled his voice. "Wait—"

Hugh pulled out his goggles and leaned back, letting out a tired sigh. "Let's just give him a minute."

"Good idea," I said, knowing those few seconds of rest could make a whole world of difference.

We heard voices of guards chatting with one another as they walked down the hall. My muscles tensed and my fingers clutched hard to the gun. Once they passed, we both relaxed again.

When neither of us said anything for a long time, I turned to look at Hugh. "We make a good team."

Hugh smiled. "I think so, too."

"Whatever happens…" I said, trying to find his eyes in

the dark. "Just make sure you look after my little sister and brother for me."

"Stop talking like that." Hugh looked through the opening again, though really just trying to avoid my eyes. "Nothing's gonna happen."

"I told Ethan you were one of my closest friends," I went on, ignoring him. "But that's not true anymore." He looked at me, and I held his gaze. "You've become like a brother to me, and you will always have a special place in my heart. Even if they take my memory away, again."

Hugh sighed, his soft gaze finally admitting that the odds of us getting out of there unharmed were not in our favor. "You took the words right out of my mouth."

I smiled, and he smiled back.

"Want some gum?" I offered, reaching into one of my pockets. Field agent uniforms had so many pockets.

"Where did you get gum?" Hugh asked.

"Dale's wife gave it to me at the yacht," I said, handing him a stick. But as I pulled another one for me, a folded piece of paper fell out.

"What's that?" he asked.

"Looks like a note." I unfolded the paper then pressed the button on my watch. The light came on, and I gasped.

Hugh leaned forward, alert. "What?" he asked in a hushed tone.

I pushed the earpiece into my ear with my hands shaking. "Benji, can you hear me? Benji!" I looked at Hugh, horrified. "We gotta get the connection back!"

Hugh grabbed my arm. "What happened?"

"Dale works for the Order!" I kicked the vent, sending the gate flying into the empty room. Field agents barged in.

I shot the first two in the chest, and as their body convulsed with the electricity, I jumped down and crouched behind a Catalyst machine. Hugh shot a couple more and their body collapsed on top of the others.

Hugh jumped down from the vent and took cover next to me as yet another field agent barged in, shooting at us. I peeked under the machine and aimed at his feet. I shot once, and he dropped to the floor.

Hugh ran toward the door and pressed his back against the wall. "I hear more coming," he said, risking a peek. He shot another agent then hurried back into the room.

"Benji, can you hear me?" I hurried to take cover behind the door and shot at another field agent that was running down the hall. "Benji!" I yelled, pressing into my earpiece. "Answer me!"

"Mia—" Benji's voice came back but then got cut out. "Now!"

The light suddenly turned off, and we quickly slipped on our night vision goggles. Hugh aimed his gun out the door, and I laid flat on the floor by his feet. He took one side, while I took the other. We shot at every agent in sight until all twelve were blacked out on the floor.

The red emergency light turned on, and we hurried out of the room.

"Mia...Hugh!" Benji's voice came back, loud and clear. "Are you both alright?"

"Benji!" I yelled running down the hall, next to Hugh. "Ditch Dale!"

We crossed what looked like a lobby, and another agent appeared through the door. Hugh jumped behind a sofa while I took cover behind a desk.

"Did you hear me?" I yelled, real gunshots hitting the steel against my back. "Dale's been reporting to the Order!"

The sound of electricity echoed down the hall then an agent dropped with a loud thud.

"Got him," Hugh said, jumping back to his feet.

I rolled out from behind the desk. "We need to split up," I said, keeping my gun in front of me. "You take the left, and I'll take the right."

Hugh pressed his lips together as if debating. I could tell he wasn't crazy about the idea, but he also knew we were running out of time and had a lot of ground to cover if we were going to find Sophia.

"Fine." He pulled me into a strong embrace. "Be careful." When he let me go, we both took off running in opposite directions.

As I got to the end of the hall, I heard footsteps coming and crouched with my back against the wall. As a man in a suit appeared around the corner, the red lights reflected off of his desperate expression.

"I found Hemsworth," I announced, jumping in front of him. Hemsworth tried to flee but I shot at the extinguisher's metal casing next to him, and he stopped.

"Don't move," I said with my teeth clenched. "Turn around and let me see your hands."

Hemsworth turned around slowly, his hands in the air as he held onto a briefcase. "Mia, please let me go."

"Where is Sophia?" I hissed, aiming my gun toward his face.

"I'm trying to get her to a safe place—"

"Where is she?" I yelled, gripping the trigger. "I will shoot you!"

"That's what they want, can't you see that?" he barked. "This whole thing was a trap, not only for you but for me, too. They sent me here to get the drive, but it isn't here. They are probably hoping you do shoot me."

"Why would they turn on you?"

"Because as soon as you took my kids, they wanted to use Alice as leverage to lure you back," he said, his jaw tightened in anger. "You have no idea what they're capable of. They're ruthless."

"Where is my mother?"

"She's safe."

"Where?"

He shook his head. "I can't tell you that."

"Why not?"

"Because they will catch you," he said, nonchalantly. "And when they do, I don't want them anywhere near my family. Now…" He took a step toward me, and I stepped back. "Let me protect your little sister."

"Don't play that card with me," I hissed, aiming the gun at his chest.

"I only took your mother because your father couldn't give her the life she deserved."

"Just tell me where Sophia is."

"You don't know how to protect her." His expression hardened. "I am begging you, Mia. Please. Let me get my daughter away from all of this."

I looked into his eyes and tears began to fill them. He really was frightened for her. I lowered my gun, and he let out a breath of relief.

"Thank you, Ace—" He flinched, then pressed his eyes shut.

"What did you call me?" I trailed off as my mouth dropped open. "No." I raised the gun and aimed at his chest, again. "Tell me you did not take my brother's memories. Tell me!"

Hemsworth raised his hands, defensively. "Mia, listen—"

"Wasn't it enough to just kill him?" I yelled, blinking the tears away and fighting the urge to pull the trigger three times. My hands were shaking. "God, I should kill you right now!"

"Your brother is alive!"

His voice echoed off the walls, and my head began to spin. "What?" My voice was barely audible.

"After I took his memory, I convinced the Order to let him go," Hemsworth said. "We thought he might've known about the journal, but the poor kid didn't know anything."

"You're lying."

"I'm not." He peered into my eyes, he was so convincing. "Not only is he safe, but he's happy. I made sure of that."

"Why would you do that for him?"

Hemsworth shrugged. "He's Alice's kid. It was the least I could do."

My heart burned in my chest like it was set on fire, but I sucked back the tears. "Where is he?"

Hemsworth bit his bottom lip. "Don't drag him back into this, Mia."

The building begun to shake and I was thrown to the floor; so was Hemsworth. I grabbed onto the threshold of the door and held on until it stopped.

"What was that?" Hugh's voice came through the earpiece.

"An explosion on the fifth floor," Benji informed. "They planted explosives all through the building! You all have to leave, now!"

I staggered to my feet when I noticed Hemsworth pushing himself up. I heard a noise behind me and instinctively gripped my gun.

Sophia stared at me with terror in her eyes. "Mia, no!" She lunged in my direction, reaching for my gun and pointing it away from her father. I stumbled backward, and we both fell to the ground.

"Sophia, stop!"

"He knows where Mom is!" she cried. "If anything happens to him, we won't know how to find her."

Rashida appeared and pointed her gun at Hemsworth. "Where is the drive?" she hissed, anger ripping through her throat. "And don't lie to me."

Hemsworth smiled. "You're never gonna find it."

The ground began to shake again, and I held on to Sophia. Rashida jerked backward, bringing her hands to her head. Hemsworth reached for his briefcase then stopped when he caught sight of Rashida's pitch black eyes, glaring at him.

"No…" I gasped. "Rashida, no!"

I pushed Sophia off of me and lunged toward Rashida as she raised her gun toward Hemsworth. Three shots were fired as I banged her back against the wall and tackled her to the ground.

"No!" Sophia screeched a piercing scream. "Daddy!" She

rushed to her father's side as he convulsed uncontrollably. "No, Daddy, please!"

I looked back at Rashida, who was staring at the scene just as horrified as I was. "I…" She looked up at me, her eyes widened in remorse. "I didn't…" she stuttered, shaking her head. "I didn't mean to…"

Hugh came from around the corner, his eyes mirroring our terror. He looked at me. I opened my mouth to speak, but nothing came out. He rushed to Sophia's side without waiting for an explanation.

Hemsworth was already dead, and Sophia's cries pierced through my heart.

"The building has been compromised!" Benji warned with an urgent tone. "You all need to get out of there, now!"

Another wave of explosion shuddered the building. I laid flat on the floor and covered my head. The sound of glass breaking filled the air. Another emergency siren came on so loud, it shocked my brain.

"Get out of there, now!" Benji yelled. "The structure is getting weaker!"

The quaking stopped, and I staggered to my feet, holding on to the threshold for balance.

"Sophia, we have to go!" Hugh yelled over the loud noise. "Please!"

"No!" Sophia cried, clinging to her father's lifeless body. "Those agents were going to take me, Hugh! They were going to put me through the Catalyst, but Daddy didn't let them. He protected me. He risked his life for me."

"I'm sorry baby, but we have to go." Hugh tried pulling her up, but she grabbed onto her father's body even tighter.

"Love, I'm sorry." Hugh wrapped his arms around Sophia and yanked her off of her father. She ripped a screeching cry as he dragged her away by force.

Rashida looked disoriented as she managed to stand. I handed her Hemsworth's briefcase, but she hesitated.

"Come on!" I yelled, snapping her out of it. "Take it and let's go!"

Another explosion shook the building, and it threw all of us off balance. We fell to the ground, and Hugh shielded Sophia with his body. The fire extinguisher crashed to the floor, shattering glass everywhere.

I reached for Hugh and tugged at his shirt. "We have to keep moving!" I yelled, pulling him up with me.

Hugh yanked Sophia to her feet, despite the ground still shaking. He leaned against the wall, and I went back to pick up Rashida who was crawling on the floor, clinging to the briefcase.

"Take the stairs at the end of the hall," Benji instructed. "That should take you out the east wing."

I pulled Rashida up, and we staggered down the hall, following close behind Hugh. He stopped to a halt, and my chest crashed against his back. We both fell to the ground, and so did Sophia.

"Watch out!" Hugh warned just as the ceiling in front of us collapsed. I turned away, covering my face. I felt Rashida's hand grip my jacket and yank me up to my feet. Hugh did the same with Sophia.

"Go to your left," Benji said. "There should be another set of stairs by the elevator."

Hugh pulled Sophia by the hand, forcing her to keep moving. We followed behind them. Hugh kicked open the double doors that led to the stairs and darted down the steps.

I heard footsteps running down the hall and turned to look. It was a soldier. He was wearing camo clothes, and I grabbed onto my gun. I stared at his figure, focusing on the outline of his back—the recognition was almost immediate.

Ethan?

"Mia, let's go!" Rashida grabbed my jacket, but I swung my arm free.

"You go!" I urged her. "And stick to the escape plan!"

"What are you doing?"

"I don't have time to explain, just go!" I pushed her into the staircase and watched as she darted down the steps, banging the briefcase against the railing.

I turned toward Ethan's image. The figment of my imagination. The illusion I so desperately begged for. But why now? Why here?

"Mia, watch out!" Benji yelled. "There's someone on that floor with you!"

"Where?" I looked around, but there was no one else there. "Benji!" I pulled the gun up to my chin. "Where?"

"He's right in front of you!"

My eyes locked on Ethan's large back and I couldn't breathe. "Benji…" I put the gun down. "Is he...real?"

"Yes! Get out of there, Mia!"

Ethan turned around, and it felt like the next explosion was inside my chest. "Ethan?" My voice was barely above a whisper. His light brown hair was cut short and he had grown a beard, but it was still my Ethan. I started running toward him. "Ethan!"

He ran toward me just as fast I was running toward him. When our bodies collided, I grabbed on to him. He felt so firm and strong, so real.

"Oh, God!" My head started spinning, and I grabbed onto his jacket with shaky hands. "You're alive."

His firm hand gripped my throat and lifted me off the ground. I looked at him, confused.

"Ethan…" I choked. "You're hurting me."

He leaned in, and I could feel his warm breath in my ear. "Good."

CHAPTER 9

Ethan had me pinned against the wall with my feet off the ground. I coughed as I tried loosening his grip from my throat.

"Ethan..." I coughed out. "It's me."

"I know who you are," he hissed in my face, and although it was so good to hear his voice, it wasn't the gentle voice I remember. There were anger and hatred mixed in his tone.

When his blue eyes peered into mine, a wave of anxiety washed over me. His eyes looked utterly empty—no love, no attachment, no...memory.

No, no, no!

I raised my ring finger and exposed my tattoo in front of his eyes. "I'm your wife!"

"How stupid do you think I am?" he grunted. "You're lucky they want you alive; otherwise I would have killed you already."

He tightened his grip around my throat, and I struggled to breathe. I hit my knuckle on the funny bone of his elbow, and he dropped me. I gasped for air while lunging toward him and jerking my knee up into his groin. He bent forward, and I pushed him to the ground. His face contorted in pain as he brought his hands to his head. The pain didn't seem to last long, and I wondered if he had just experienced a surge.

"Ethan, they're lying to you!" I yelled over the siren that was still blaring.

He shot up a glance in my direction, rage burning in his eyes. He growled in anger and charged toward me. When he tried to punch me, I swerved.

"Ethan, stop!"

He threw another punch, and I swerved again. When he swung another, I ducked and added a blow to his side. He winced, and that slowed his momentum, but not by much. He was tall and strong and very, very resilient.

"I don't want to hurt you!"

"Then that makes one of us," he spoke through his clenched teeth, charging at me, again. He grabbed my wrist and twisted my arm to my back. I elbowed his stomach then his face. He jerked back but didn't let go. He turned my arm even further, and I bit back a scream. I jumped on the wall in front of me and did a backflip, taking Ethan's arm with me and shoving his forearm into his own neck.

While behind him, I reached for the gun on his belt. He elbowed my stomach, and I jerked back. He turned around, now more annoyed than angry and swung another punch toward my face. I blocked his blow with my forearm and grimaced. His agility was ridiculously polished, and his moves were so quick and skillful.

Ethan got hold of my neck and threw me with my back

against a glass medicine cabinet. It shattered behind me, and I felt it pierce through my flesh. I kicked him in the stomach and fell to the ground with thick liquid sliding down my back. I looked up and saw Ethan marching toward me again.

"Stop!" I pulled out the gun I had taken from him and aimed it at his chest. I pushed myself up, and we stood facing each other, struggling to keep our breathing steady.

"Ethan…" I looked into his eyes with a soft and gentle gaze, but it did nothing to soften his solid rock demeanor. He stared at me with his jaw tightened, and his fists clenched into a ball. There was so much hatred in his eyes, but where was it all coming from? I could understand why he wouldn't remember me, but to hate me like that?

I lowered the gun. "I don't want to hurt you."

Ethan charged again. He rammed his shoulder into my stomach, lifted me up, then threw me to the ground. My back burned and I dropped the gun. He raised his thick boot toward my face, but I rolled out from under him. I reached for my taser gun, but he stepped on my hand just as I pulled the trigger. The taser bullet hit the outlet on the wall, and a sudden spark blew out, consuming all of the broken vials on the floor. The blue and purple light of the fire spread within seconds, swallowing the walls.

Ethan dropped to his knees, his eyes widened in fright. He gripped the floor, trying to steady himself. Was he terrified of fires?

I dropped the gun and charged in his direction, adrenaline pumping through my veins. When our bodies collided, I hooked my arms under his and lifted him up off the ground, all the while running toward the window. I covered my face, using Ethan's body as a shield. The glass shattered against his muscular back.

In midair, I braced myself for the impact. I felt the whiplash of branches hitting my body. We hit the ground at an incline and started to roll down the hill. My body hit against rocks and logs until it crashed against a large boulder. Every muscle in my body was throbbing. I opened my eyes, the sun had already started to rise. I reached for a canoe that was turned upside-down by the edge of the river and pulled myself up.

"Ethan?" I looked toward the rapids, and Ethan's body was flowing down the river, being dragged by the strong current. "Ethan!" He was trying to swim but was using only one of his arms. He looked injured.

"Ethan, hold on!" I flipped the canoe right-side-up. "I'm coming!" I pushed it toward the water but the cut on my back burned and I dropped to my knees. "I'm coming!" I staggered back to my feet, biting back the stabbing pain that shot up my back. It took all I had to push the canoe into the water. Once the canoe got momentum, I grabbed the paddles from the ground and jumped inside.

The canoe got hit by a strong wave, and I held on. "Ethan!" I could see his jacket floating above water, being carried down the rapids. I paddled toward him as fast as I could. The current was strong and violent. The waves crashed onto the canoe at every side, it was hard to keep control.

"Ethan, grab the boat!" I yelled, trying to get the canoe as close to him as possible. I extended the paddle to him. "Ethan, grab the paddle!"

He didn't make any effort to reach for it.

"Ethan, grab it!" I hit him with the paddle, and he raised his head out of the water, gasping for air. "Grab the paddle!"

When his head went under water again, I threw the paddle aside and reached for him with my bare hands. I grabbed onto his camo jacket and tried pulling him up, but he was too heavy for me, and my back was still burning. I stopped and watched the waves for a few seconds—when it hit the canoe again, I used its impact to lift Ethan up out of the water and into the boat.

He fell on the floor of the canoe, coughing out all the water he'd swallowed. I went back to paddling and trying to control the boat. The current had gotten much stronger as I tried to swerve away from the rocks. Ethan held on to the front of the canoe with one arm, while with the other he put pressure on the side of his stomach.

Finally, the current slowed and I dropped the paddle with shaky hands. I leaned back, exhausted. We were still being taken downstream but no longer at a fierce pace. I looked at Ethan. He was lying on the opposite end of the canoe, facing me.

"I can't believe you're alive," I breathed, trying not to cry.

Ethan's eyes were barely opened, and his breathing was weak. I scanned his body and only then did I notice he had a tree branch pierced into the side of his stomach.

I gasped, jumping to my feet. "Ethan, you're bleeding!"

"Don't..." he hissed, holding his side with both of his hands, trying to put as much pressure on the wound as he could.

I leaned toward him. "Let me help—"

"Don't touch me," he growled.

"I just saved your life," I snapped. "I'm not going to hurt you, just let me take a look." I reached for him, again.

"No." He stopped me. "I know what you want…" he trailed off, running out of breath.

"I want to help you—"

"You want to take me with you and finish what you started. They told me this would happen…" he sounded tired. "They told me you would come for me.."

I crouched in front of him and searched for his eyes. "Ethan, they're lying to you."

He shook his head, pain contorting his expression. "They told me you would say that."

"Look!" I raised my tattoo for him to see. "You have one, too. It's our wedding band."

He kept shaking his head. "That only means that we were part of the same squad years ago. The squad that you betrayed and got everyone killed. And now you're here to finish me off."

"Ethan, none of that is true."

"I remember everything!" he barked but then grunted in pain. "I remember you setting fire to my bunker and locking me inside."

I stared at him, completely at a loss as to how to persuade him to believe me over his own memories.

"Those memories aren't real," I tried, anyway. "It's a simulation."

He coughed and I could tell speaking was becoming difficult for him. He was bleeding too much, too fast.

"If you don't let me help you," I said, my voice cracking, "you're going to bleed out."

"So be it," he breathed.

"Ethan, please."

He forced his eyes open and looked at me. "I rather die from this than be killed by you." He reached for the branch and yanked it out in one hard pull.

"No!" I jumped onto him and pressed both of my hands down on his wound. Blood gushed out of the opening like an overflowing gutter. I pushed down harder, but it was passing through my fingers.

"Stop." Ethan kept trying to push my hands away. Even bleeding out he was stronger than me. "Get your hands off me." He grabbed my shirt and threw me out of the canoe.

I hung onto the side of the canoe and climbed back into it, soaking wet. Ethan huffed, looking away from me, but then his eyes rolled back and his hands dropped.

I jumped on him again, pressing into his wound. He winced, barely able to open his eyes. When our eyes locked, I couldn't fight back the tears.

"No…" I reached for the flare gun that was in the compartment under the wooden seat and pointed toward the sky. Ethan's focus came back to me.

"I am not losing you again," I said, pulling the trigger.

The flare lit up the soft blue sky, and within seconds several field agents appeared on both sides of the river, holding up their guns and aiming them at me.

CHAPTER 10

I SAT BAREFOOTED on the white tile floor with my back against the wall. It was a white padded wall like a nut house, except they didn't have me in a strait jacket. They did give me white scrubs to put on after stripping me off of everything, including my shoes.

The door swung open, and a male nurse with spiky brown hair walked in wearing a white mask over his nose and mouth. He reached for my arm. I grabbed his wrist, twisting to his back, then wrapped my arm around his throat.

"Where is Ethan?" I demanded, keeping my voice low.

"Don't worry about him," he said in a hushed tone. "Take my access card and leave this place."

"Who are you?"

"Matt," he whispered. "I know Rashida."

When I didn't respond, he urged, "Hurry before someone else comes."

"Where is Ethan?" I asked, again.

"Are you crazy—"

I tightened my grip around his throat. "Where is he?"

"Exam room 9," he choked out. "Now, you need to leave—"

I pressed my arm tighter around his neck, pushing his head down just enough to cut off his blood flow. When he passed out, I eased his body to the floor. The mask fell from his face, and I noticed he looked a lot younger than most nurses I'd seen. There was something about him that reminded me of Victor. It could've been his age, or maybe his haircut.

I touched two fingers to the side of his throat to make sure he still had a pulse. He did. I reached for his access card and taser then headed out the door.

When I finally found room 9, I looked through the small rectangle window on the door and saw Ethan sleeping. The room was dark, and there were no windows. I stepped inside then shut the door behind me. The dim light from the hall pierced through the glass, bathing the room in a soft glow. I leaned my back against the door and sighed as I stared at Ethan's peaceful face. He was lying shirtless on a gurney in the far corner of the room. His stomach was wrapped with a large roll of gauze. He had a bag of IV attached to his arm. The heart monitor beeped at a regular rhythm—though survival was part of the military training, it wasn't too detailed on medical procedures.

Ethan was alive, that's all that mattered.

I stepped closer, trying to be as quiet as I could. There was another bag hanging down the metal hook, also attached to his vein. The label said it was some type of painkiller.

The bandage on the side of his stomach was turning crimson. He was bleeding. I reached for it and removed it, slowly. When I finally pulled it off, I had to hold back a gasp. It was getting infected. I threw the bandage aside and walked over to the medicine cabinet. I scanned through the vials, trying to remember the names of the plants Dale had shown me.

No, they weren't liquid. I moved to the next cabinet and found the stash of creams. I reached for the aloe, then the blagleek... parsnip... adronna. I scooped a bit of each into a metal container and mixed them together with my finger. I wiped it on my pants then reached for a pair of latex gloves before picking up the metal container and bringing it to Ethan's side. As I watched him sleep, my heart throbbed. I knew I had missed him but having him so close again, I just couldn't fathom how I ever managed to live without him.

As much as I wanted to stand there and watch him for the rest of the night, I knew I was running out of time. Matt would be waking up soon and no doubt, he would have to sound the alarm.

I turned my focus back to Ethan's wound and started to apply the shield tulsi cream. I tried to be gentle, yet I knew I had to hurry. I used as much of the cream as I could but couldn't keep my heart from melting at the sensation of touching his skin. It was warm and soft, and I wanted to feel so much more of him.

The cream was all gone, but I couldn't bring myself to stop rubbing on him. What if that were the last time I would ever get to touch him? The thought scared me more than anything and I—

Ethan grabbed my wrist, and I jumped, startled. The

metal container splattered on the floor and Ethan hurried to his feet, twisting me around and pressing my back into his chest.

"What did you do to me?" he hissed, pressing his lips to my ear as he wrapped his fingers around my throat. Part of me knew I should've been scared but feeling the warmth of his breath against my skin felt so comforting.

"Your wound was infected. That cream should help it heal more quickly," I said, making no effort to fight back. "It's called shield tulsi."

Although I couldn't see Ethan's face, I could tell by his breathing that he was looking at all the different creams I'd left open on top of the tray.

His breathing returned to my ear. "Why are you here?"

"I needed to see you," I said simply. "I needed to know you were okay."

Even though he didn't respond, I could hear his breathing slow—as well as his heartbeat against my back.

"If I wanted to hurt you," I said, keeping my voice soft and unthreatening. "I would've done it by now."

He softened his grip around my throat but still didn't respond.

"I would never hurt you," I assured him. "I love you."

A painful grunt ripped through his throat, and he pushed me away from him. When I turned around, he had his hands on his head. I gasped as a flame of hope ignited inside me.

"You remembered something, didn't you?" Though it sounded like a question, I'd intended as a statement. I could tell he had a surge. I took a step toward him, but he raised a hand to stop me.

"Enough." He looked up to meet my eyes. I stared at his angry but still, beautiful figure. "I don't wanna hear another word."

The door swung open, and we both glanced toward Matt who stood motionless, staring at us.

"Don't move!" Matt ordered, raising a taser at me. "Hands behind your back!"

I looked at Ethan, feeling a sudden urge to cry. Just the thought of being away from him again, made my heart ache.

Ethan leaned back on the gurney, keeping his head low as he reached for a new bandage.

Another male nurse showed up, and I placed both hands behind my back. When Matt finally cuffed me, the other nurse took out a syringe while pulling up my sleeve. I recognized the clear serum, and it felt exactly the same as it did all the other times it was shoved into my vein. It was cold at first, then it paralyzed me.

* * *

An hour later, after the Catalyst machine finished running for the third time, my memories were still intact.

"What happened?" a man yelled into the intercom, his voice furious.

"Mr. Sadykov—"

"Why didn't it work?" the man yelled. Apparently, Sadykov was his name.

"We don't know, sir." One of the nurses responded, terrified. "But we'll keep trying."

"Then get to it!"

After the fifth attempt with no success, I heard the door being kicked open. I was pulled out of the machine, and when I opened my eyes, a balled man with big dark eyes towered over me. His squared jaw was tight while his nostrils flared with rage. He grabbed a fist full of my hair.

"Why isn't it working?" he hissed. It was the same voice from the intercom.

I didn't respond. The drug still had me feeling numb, and the sensation traveled up and down my stomach. I tried to focus on my breathing so that I didn't vomit.

"She can't talk, sir," one of the nurses spoke from behind him. Sadykov glared over his shoulder.

"Is that right?" Sadykov replied with a sinister tone and the nurse swallowed hard. "Then, perhaps you can answer my question."

"Maybe... it's the machine, sir," the nurse said, nervously.

"The machine?" Sadykov echoed. The nurse began to sweat. "Very well, then." Sadykov signaled someone else into the room. "Take the girl out and put him in it. Let's see if the machine is really the problem."

The nurse cried in a panic as he was grabbed by field agents.

Matt rushed to my side, but just as he was about to inject me with the mobility serum, Sadykov pushed him out of the way, an angry growl ripping through his throat. He grabbed me by my hair and turned my head toward him.

"I am going to ask you one more time..." he hissed. "Why isn't it working?"

When I didn't respond, he pulled my hair and hit my head against the cot. I closed my eyes, waiting for the pain of the blow but it never came. I was still numb from the serum. I grunted anyway, pretending I'd felt it. When I opened my eyes, Sadykov looked pleased.

"You have no idea what I'm capable of," he whispered, his jaw tight. "I strongly suggest you don't tempt me."

I tried to speak, but I couldn't move my mouth. My voice, however, was audible. "Give my husband his real memories back... and I'll give you what you want."

Sadykov leaned in, tightening his grip on my hair. "You don't call the shots here," he spat back. "I do!" He slapped the cot above my head then stepped back. "Pull her up!"

The nurses rushed to unstrap me. Sadykov pointed to a chair across the room, and they dragged me to it. As they were about to strap my arms, Sadykov stopped them.

"Get me the taser stick," he said, turning to Matt—his eyes widened in terror as the blood drained from his face. "What's wrong with you, kid?"

The door opened, and Ethan walked in, his expression emotionless. "Here you go." Ethan held up a white stick with a U at the end. That was the taser. Beads of sweat started to form on my forehead, and I swallowed hard.

"Looking good, soldier." Sadykov slapped Ethan on the arm then turned to face me. "Now, where were we? Oh, yeah..." He stepped forward with a wicked smile.

Matt closed his eyes and looked away as I started to scream. The other nurse reached for a white cloth and tied it around my mouth. I bit down on it as soon as I began to regain the slightest sense of mobility.

Sadykov's wicked grin grew wider. "Let's see if we can get you talking, shall we?"

* * *

I WOKE up to a white popcorn ceiling. I was lying on a gurney, but I wasn't in the same room as before. A large white curtain surrounded the small space I was in. I tried turning on my side, but every movement felt so excruciating it made it hard to breathe.

The effect of the serum was long gone, and I felt every burn the taser had marked into my skin. Even my throat was burning, but that had to do with how much I'd screamed. I couldn't even imagine what it would've felt like had Sadykov figured out I wasn't feeling the full force and ordered for the mobility serum to be injected for the second half of the torture.

The curtain was pushed open and my body tensed.

"Oh, thank God you're okay." Matt let out a sigh of relief. "I knew you were stubborn but suicidal is a little much, don't you think?"

"Excuse me?" I tried pushing myself up, but it hurt too much.

"You shouldn't move," he said, touching my arm as he reached for the metal container on top of the counter. It wasn't until I felt his touch on my bare skin that I realized I wasn't wearing a shirt. I touched my top and felt my bra.

"Where am I?" I asked.

"The medical wing," he said in a hushed tone, putting the metal container on the gurney next to me. "I'll leave the door unlocked, and you can leave tonight."

"I'm not going anywhere."

"Unbelievable," he mumbled, slipping on a pair of latex gloves. He reached for the sheet and pulled it out of his way. I winced as I peeked down to make sure I still had pants on. They also had burn marks all over.

"It's going to sting a bit," Matt said. "You can bite down on the sheet if you need to."

I lay my head back down on the pillow and sucked in a breath. "Just get it over with," I said.

Matt dug three fingers into the container and scooped out the cream. As he began to apply on each burn, I closed my eyes and suppressed the nausea that came with the pain. Another shot of that numb serum would've been great right now.

The smell of the cream grew stronger, and I suddenly recognized it. "Is that shield tulsi?" I asked, looking up at him. "How did you find out about it?"

"Why does it matter?"

"Was Dale really working for the Order?"

"Yes," Matt said. "But don't worry. Rashida and them ditched him."

"Where is he now?"

"Running from the Order." Matt stopped. "That's all there is to do once you fail them. That's why I'm begging you. Please, let me help you escape."

"Not without Ethan."

"God!" Matt grunted. "How much beating is it gonna take for you to realize that Ethan is not the same!"

"What is your problem?"

"Forget it." He shook his head, scooping more cream on

his fingers and treating the last few burns. I grimaced at his touch. "I'm almost done," he added.

When the curtain moved, I glanced toward the sound. An older man with white hair and a clean-cut beard walked in. He was holding a brown paper bag.

"Matt..." the man said, holding the curtain open. "Will you excuse us, please?"

Matt nodded, but I could tell by the look in his eyes he didn't want to leave. He walked to the trash can, yanked one glove at a time then tossed it. It wasn't until he walked to the sink and started to wash his hands that I realized he was stalling.

Oh, God. He was going to get himself killed.

I pushed myself up despite the pain then reached for the bed sheet to cover myself with it. "What do you want?" I asked, looking at the white-haired man.

He turned to me, his expression soft. "For starters, I brought you some food." He placed the paper bag on top of the metal tray then turned to Matt. He didn't have to ask again. Matt rushed out with his hands still damp. The man turned back to me. "I heard you like Chinese."

"I'm not hungry."

"I'm sorry we got off on the wrong foot," he said. "My name is Ted Warren." He offered a small smile, but it wasn't nearly enough to put me at ease.

"What do you want?" I asked, again.

"You look so much like your mother." He stared in admiration. "She was one of the brightest minds I've ever encountered. In all my years in this field, I've never met anyone so bright, so caring, and so magnificently beautiful as she was."

I clung to the sheet wrapped around me. I hated that he knew my mother more than I did.

"When she told me about her idea for the Catalyst trial, I thought it was genius—"

"Is that why you ripped it out from under her?"

"I did no such thing. We were a team. In fact, your mother handpicked each one of us. I know…" He chuckled. "I have no idea what she was thinking, either. Personally, I didn't think it was going to work. We were all so different. But your mother, as always, knew what she was doing. Sadykov always had a strong personality. He intimidated others which gave your mother a sense of confidence to have him by her side. I, on the other hand, like to think things through and look at it from different angles. Hemsworth was very good with people, which came in handy when trying to get funding. Overall, we made a great team. It was a terrible tragedy when we lost her."

"Don't pretend you cared about her," I spoke through my clenched teeth. "Hemsworth ripped her away from her family, and none of you did anything about it."

"We had no idea what he'd done to Alice until recently. Though I can't say I was surprised, he had always been in love with her."

"Is that why you wanted him killed?" I asked. "Because he hid my mother from you?"

"We didn't want him killed. I even tried to warn him, but…of course, he wouldn't listen." Warren shook his head. "Can't blame him. They took his daughter. That's what they do. They use family as leverage because they know it works."

"Why do you keep saying they?"

Warren looked at me. "Believe it or not, the Order is not the enemy."

"Then, who is?"

"Who do you think we work for?" Warren asked, taking a seat at the edge of the bed. "On our last presentation—at the fundraiser—the president was very impressed by the demonstration. But instead of just funding our department, he asked us to use it on the soldiers. I tried to explain that the trial wasn't ready for something like that, but he insisted."

"My mother would never have agreed to that."

"We weren't given a choice. If we declined his offer, he would've taken the department from us and placed it in the hands of God-knows-who. At least, this way there's still hope we get it back to its original purpose. Besides..." He shrugged. "That president was about to leave office so we didn't think it would last. We weren't counting on Conor Bates taking charge."

"You mean the Vice President?"

Warren nodded. "He was purposely given the VP position to keep the new president in the dark while keeping the trial running."

"So, the new president doesn't know about the trial?"

Warren shook his head. "I've tried to get an audience with him, but when Conor found out, he used my grandkids as leverage to make sure I never tried that again."

"Was Conor the one who tried having Ethan killed in the fire?" I asked, curious.

"No. The fire was Hemsworth's idea," Warren paused, his demeanor disturbed. "No one was supposed to get hurt. He was just trying to scare you. He even arranged for that fake call from the hospital—he wanted to make sure you got out. He had no idea Ethan wasn't going to be with you, and when we heard that both your husband and your brother had died, we called for a meeting immediately. That's why we were at his mansion that night. Things were spiraling out of control, and we wanted it to stop."

"Then why order the beating on Hugh?"

Warren sighed. "Sadykov is a very disturbed man, which makes him very emotionally unstable. When Hugh's father took his job and became your mother's new right hand, Sadykov developed an extreme hatred for the guy. That night wasn't about Hugh, at all."

"What about Ethan?" I asked. "Who took him?"

"We did."

"Why?" I pressed. "To get to me?"

"It wasn't about you," he said. "We had already decided to leave you alone. Why else do you think you were able to live next door to Hemsworth and not be caught?"

"Then, why Ethan?"

"He took something from us. When he broke into the Fort Benning facility, he didn't just take your file. He uploaded the whole drive which contained every detail of the Catalyst trial. Details that could compromise all of us."

"How do you know it was him?"

"We had you followed," Warren confessed. "According to Dr. Greene, you were starting to remember things so we were hoping you would lead us to the missing pages of the journal. Once we found out Ethan was still alive, we kept tabs on him, too."

I couldn't believe it. Ethan was taken from Cooper

Creek. He was never a figment of my imagination. Everything, that whole time, was real.

I shook my head, forcing myself to focus. "What about the drive?" I asked.

"After he hid it, he took a drug that made him forget the previous 12-hours," Warren spoke with almost a growl. "That's why I'm here, Mia. I need that drive, and you're the only one who can get it."

"How come?"

"Seems that ever since Ethan saw you again, he's been having surges, which means his memories are coming back," Warren explained. "I need you to get him to remember where he hid the drive."

"And why would I help you?"

"Because the information on that drive compromises all of us," Warren said, firmly. "And I don't mean just the Order. I mean your mother, Rashida, Hugh, Benji, and everyone who has ever been connected with this trial. We will all go to prison."

"What do you plan to do with the drive?" I asked.

"Destroy it," he said, firmly. "I will not go to prison for someone else's mistake, and I'm sure you don't want your mother to pay that price, either. Besides, you and I both know that in her condition, she will not survive in there."

"So, what exactly do you need from me?" I asked.

"Whatever it takes," Warren said. "We need Ethan to remember where the drive is."

"It would speed the process if you just tell Ethan who I really am."

"Fair enough." Warren stood. "I'll tell him everything as soon he's done with his assignment."

"What assignment?"

Warren let out a chuckle. "We're all puppets of the VP, Mia. That includes your precious husband. Anyway, there's a shower in that bathroom and food in the bag," he said, loosening his tie. "You can sleep here tonight, and I'll have Ethan come get you in the morning."

"What if I can't make him remember?" I asked, pushing through the knot in my throat.

Warren offered a small smile. "You already have."

CHAPTER 11

I TOOK A LUKEWARM shower, but my skin was still burning. I padded each burn down with the towel, it was itching like crazy. I slipped into the camo pants Matt left for me but couldn't find the green shirt that went with it.

I walked out of the bathroom wearing my bra, leaving the light on to illuminate the dark clinic as I snooped into the cabinets. I grimaced as I crouched down to open the bottom cabinets. Did I even want a shirt? I touched my skin to see how sensitive the burns felt to the touch and it was still very sore. I tried scratching around it, but it hurt.

After searching through a second time, I decided to give up and wait to ask Matt in the morning. I went back to the bathroom and turned off the light. I grabbed a bottled water from the mini fridge in the corner and opened it on my way back to bed. I felt so ridiculously awake; it made me nervous. If I went without any sleep for twenty-four hours, the mindlock would deactivate.

When I pushed the curtain aside, someone slammed into me so hard it made my head spin. I lost my balance and stumbled to the ground. The pain that shot through my body was so excruciating it made me want to gag. I closed my eyes and focused on my breathing.

"Where the heck were you?" It was Ethan's voice. "Where did you go?" he asked again, his voice firm.

"I was in the shower." I whimpered as I ached. "What are you doing here?"

He cleared his throat. "I was told to check on you."

"In the middle of the night?"

"Get up."

I tried, but it was too painful.

"Oh, for goodness sakes." Ethan crouched impatiently and scooped me up off the floor. He wasn't particularly gentle, but he wasn't aggressive, either. It wasn't until he laid me down on the gurney that I realized I'd stopped breathing.

"I didn't mean to knock you down," he said as some form of apology, though still distant. "When I didn't see you, I thought you had run away."

I reached for his hand. "I'm not going anywhere."

He pulled back and shoved both hands into his pockets. "How are your burns?"

"Better," I said. "How is your wound?"

"Healed."

"Did it leave a scar?"

"Yes."

I glanced at his stomach. "Can I see?"

He looked at me with a soft expression, and I was

surprised that he was actually considering it. But then, his face hardened again. "No."

I sighed. It would've been nice to touch him again. I sat up and reached for the remaining tulsi cream in the metal container on top of the tray. "Would you mind helping me?"

Ethan's eyes widened. "Why can't you do it?"

"I can't reach the ones on my back," I said, turning around and showing it to him. "And I can't see the ones on my neck, either."

He stared at the container, hesitantly. "Fine, but only the ones you can't reach." He took the bowl from my hand and stood like a statue waiting for me to get in position.

I turned around and leaned against the bed. "Do you need more light?"

"No, this is fine." He scooped some of the cream and applied to the first burn. When I shivered, he stopped. "What's wrong?"

"Nothing," I said. "It's just... itching."

When he moved on to the next burn, he rubbed it in a circle, scratching it lightly with his finger. I closed my eyes and felt my body relax. He took his time moving from one burn to the next, and I had to gasp for air. I hadn't felt his touch on my skin since we made love back in the loft, before the fire.

"The Order is not as bad as you think," he said, his voice soft behind me.

"They tortured me, Ethan."

He stopped rubbing, but only for a moment. "I know."

"Have you done that?" I asked, turning around to face

him. We were so close I was expecting him to step back, but he didn't. "Tortured someone, I mean?"

"Yes," he said, lifting my chin then scooping more cream for the burns on my neck.

"Don't you think that's inhumane?"

"When I was in China with my team, we slipped up and got caught." He breathed, and I felt his warmth on my collarbone. "They tortured every single one of my men right in front of me, and in ways that I can't even say it aloud without my stomach churning. You want to talk about inhumane..."

"Those memories aren't real," I whispered, reaching to touch his face. "I know you're in there."

He backed away. "Stop that."

"You know as well as I do that every flash of memory you have, doesn't match the man you're describing."

I stared into his light blue eyes and just as I thought I was getting through to him, he broke my gaze.

"You should get some sleep." He threw the metal container back on the tray and stepped back. "I'll be back in the morning."

"What will it take for you to believe me?"

He stopped just short of the curtain but didn't turn around. "I never said I didn't."

**

THE NEXT MORNING, I woke up with Ethan throwing a white shirt on my face. It wasn't the most romantic awakening but having him be the first person I saw when I opened my eyes was all I could ask for amidst all that nightmare.

Ethan turned his back to me.

"At ease soldier," I teased. "There's nothing here you haven't seen before."

"Are you done?"

"Just about." I slipped into the shirt and already could tell the burns felt much better. "Where can I get a toothbrush?"

"Everything you need is in the bathroom." Ethan held the curtain opened for me then waited at the door like a bodyguard. "Hurry up."

"You used to be more patient," I said, brushing my hair. It had already grown down to the middle of my back. I was in desperate need of a haircut.

After I finished brushing my teeth, Ethan swung me around, his grip firm on my arm. "When you go in there, do as they say." His lips were so close to mine, I could almost taste him. "Understood?"

I nodded, fighting against the urge to pull him into me. "Yes."

"Good." He ripped the brush from my hand and threw it across the bathroom. "Let's go."

Ethan pushed open the double doors that led outside, and I shivered. The temperature had dropped significantly since the last time I was out. Groups of soldiers marched by, flawlessly in sync. They wore thick camo jackets as they marched toward the mountains for training. A wind blew past us, and I wrapped my arms around myself.

"Can I have a jacket?"

"Don't be a wimp—" Ethan stopped to a halt as a harsh

grunt ripped through his throat. He shut his eyes as his face hardened. I touched his shoulder, knowing he was having another surge.

"Breathe," I said. "It usually helps."

He lifted his head slowly, taking in deep breaths. "Keep walking."

"I don't know the way."

Ethan grunted as he pushed himself forward. I sped up, trying to keep up with his long strides. "Where are we going?" I asked.

"Warren asked to see you."

I stopped and crossed my arms. "What if I don't want to go?"

Ethan pointed to the row of cabins in the distance, then at the camera on the edge of the roof. "They have eyes everywhere."

"They're watching us, right now?"

"Most likely."

I turned to the camera and raised the back of my hand, but as I was about to offer a not-so-nice sign, Ethan grabbed my arm and pushed it down.

"What is wrong with you?" he hissed. "Do you want to get yourself killed?"

"I'm not afraid of them."

"It's not them you should be afraid of." He gripped my wrist and twisted it so I could see the burns on my skin. "Some people will make this look like child's play."

"They already took everything from me." I leaned in, inches from his face. "At least my dignity I get to keep."

"I'll make sure to carve that on your gravestone."

"Since when do you care what happens to me?"

He clenched his jaw. "I don't."

"Liar."

He slapped my hand away and kept walking. "Just don't say anything stupid and you'll be fine."

"You don't have to babysit me."

"Then act like it." He stopped just short of the door and again jerked forward, grimacing. Though the pain of the surge twisted his face, he held his composure.

"Ethan—"

He let out a frustrated grunt then reached for the doorknob. He yanked it so hard I was surprised it didn't break off the door.

He led me down a long hallway, and when we turned the corner, Warren was walking out of a room with a man next to him. I'd seen him before. He was tall and slim, had short blonde hair and was wearing a suit. Two guards stood behind him.

"Isn't that the vice president?" I whispered to Ethan.

"That's none of your business," Ethan whispered back. "Stay here." He pushed me against the wall then walked toward Warren.

"You're right." A young woman in her late twenties peeked out of the exam room behind me. "That is the vice president, but don't get too close."

"What are you here for?" I asked.

"A physical," she said, leaning on the threshold of the door. "Apparently, it's needed to keep working at the white house."

"Here is the man of the hour," Warren announced as he introduced Ethan. "He's the best we've got."

"He better be." The vice president gripped Ethan's hand in a firm handshake. "We can't afford any mistakes."

"There will be no mistake, sir," Ethan assured.

"I hope for your sake that you're right," the vice president said, still gripping Ethan's hand. "If anything goes wrong, my backup plan will shoot you on sight. Do you understand?"

"Yes, sir."

My stomach twisted at the thought of anyone shooting Ethan and I caught Warren glancing at me. He wanted me to hear that. Could Warren have been telling the truth? Were they mere puppets in the hand of the government?

"Very good, then." The vice president let go of Ethan's hand and turned to Warren. "Oh, and make sure she's all set for that...physical," he added, pointing toward the woman who was still standing by the exam room. When he looked at her, she lowered her head and wrapped her arms around herself. She was scared of him.

Warren's jaw tightened. "Anything else?"

"Ask me that again in a week," the vice president said with a charming wink, but Warren didn't even crack a smile.

The vice president signaled for his bodyguards to follow him down the hall and I lowered my head as they all walked by. He stopped in front of the woman and gently tucked a strand of hair behind her ear. "I'll see you back at work soon." When he brushed her cheek, her hands started to shake. Still, she forced a smile.

Two nurses suddenly approached. "Ready, ma'am?" one of them asked through his mask. The woman nodded. "This way, please."

The vice president watched her go, his eyes suddenly falling on me. "Oh, hi. I don't think I've had the pleasure," he said with a seductive smile. "I'm Conor." He offered his hand, and I took it.

"Mia."

"Mia..." he echoed, rubbing his soft thumb over the back of my hand. "A beautiful name for a beautiful woman."

His light eyes sparkled, and his dimples were beyond charming, but when his cold wedding ring touched my skin, it made my stomach turn.

"Warren is ready for you," Ethan spoke in a thunderous voice. "Now." He ripped me away from the vice president's touch and practically dragged me down the hall. "What was that all about?" he hissed.

"He sexually assaulted that woman, didn't he?" I asked, keeping my voice low.

"She's just one of many," Ethan whispered back. "Now, stay away from him." He pushed me into the room, and I ran into the table.

"Ms. Hunter," Warren greeted from across the room. "Nice of you to join us."

Ethan stepped inside and closed the door behind him. I looked around at all the monitors covering the walls. One in particular at the center was larger than the others. It showed footage that looked familiar—a construction site but in the middle of a forest. No, it wasn't a forest. It was an island—

Sadykov pressed a button on the panel, and the screen turned off.

Warren turned to Ethan. "Major."

Ethan stepped forward. "Sir."

"Go make sure everything is ready," Warren ordered. "And make some room for Mia. She'll be going with you."

"Yes, sir."

My heart began to race with anxiety when Ethan left and closed the door behind him. Even though he was no longer the Ethan I'd married, I still felt safer with him.

Once the door clicked shut, Warren turned to me. "So, have you thought about it?"

"I did, and I'll help you find the drive," I said, "but under one condition."

Warren leaned back against the control panel. "I'm listening."

"I give you the drive, and you give Ethan his memories back, then let both of us go."

Warren nodded. "If that's what you want, that's fine. But perhaps, you would consider a different option." He offered a smile. "Maybe you might like to join us."

"Join you?" I laughed. "Please, humor me."

"We both want the same thing, Mia."

"I want to shut down the Catalyst trial."

"Do you really want to destroy everything your mother worked so hard to build?" Warren asked. "The vision your mother had for this project was sensational, and in the right hands it can be revolutionary."

"What are you saying?"

"I'm saying..." He crossed his arms, making himself comfortable. "Once we take Conor out and restore the trial to its intended purpose, we would like for you to take your mother's place in the Order. Help us honor her legacy."

I stared at Warren, speechless.

"You don't have to give us an answer right now, but please think about it."

The phone on the wall rang, and Sadykov picked it up. He nodded a few times then started to speak Russian. Once he hung up, he turned to Warren. "Conference is about to start."

"Alright, then." Warren stood up straighter and smoothed out his suit. "You find that drive, and you got yourself a deal—whichever one you choose."

"And find a jacket, those burns look hideous," Sadykov mumbled. As he passed by me, I grabbed the taser from his belt and shocked him on the back of his neck. His body shuddered violently before slamming to the ground. I sucked in a breath of satisfaction as I stared at him, temporarily defeated.

"Truth be told, I've wanted to do that for a long time," Warren said with a smile.

"What's gonna happen to that woman?" I asked, turning to face him.

He hesitated but only for a moment. "We have orders to remove only the memory of...a specific incident, then send her back to work."

"Back to him?" My stomach turned. "Why can't we help her?"

"We are helping her," Warren assured. "We're removing a very unpleasant memory from her life."

"Only to have it happen again!"

"Do you have a better idea?"

"Don't erase her memory and just let her go."

"If we do that, she'll have to spend her whole life

running, and when he catches her, which he will, he'll have her killed."

"How can you be so sure?"

"Because I've tried it," Warren said in almost a growl. "And now she's dead."

"Still…" I shook my head. "It's wrong."

"It's the less of two evils," Warren said, firmly. "We're working on a plan to get Conor out. If everything goes well, we won't have to put up with this any longer. Now, let's go before Sadykov wakes up."

CHAPTER 12

*E*THAN PARKED in front of a hotel and jumped out of the jeep, leaving the key in the ignition for the valet. The hotel was an elegant high-rise with a red carpet leading up the steps to a doorman. Ethan and I wore military pants with a plain white shirt.

"Hurry up," Ethan said, impatiently.

"You still haven't told me what we're doing here," I said jumping out of the jeep and walking around the car.

"I already told you, the president will be giving a peace treaty speech with the Chinese president in a few days regarding ending the war," Ethan said, reaching for his bag in the backseat. "They're going to set up a podium outside the opera house across the street, and Conor wants to make sure no rooms are available on this hotel for that date."

"Why?" I asked, walking up the steps next to him.

"Because..." Ethan offered a gesture of gratitude to the doorman as he opened the door for us. "The president gets hundreds of threats, every day."

"Still doesn't explain what I'm doing here," I said, hitting the small silver bell at the front desk. The ring was so loud it startled the concierge who was on the phone.

"I'll be right there," he said, glancing over his shoulder. He typed in the computer for a few more seconds then came over. "How can I help you?"

"We have a reservation," Ethan said pulling out his ID. "Ethan Stadler."

Of course, they gave him a fake name.

The concierge typed in the computer, again. "I'm sorry, there is no reservation under that name."

"Can you check one more time?" Ethan asked.

The man typed Ethan's name a second time. "Nothing, sir."

"Try Mia Hunter," I cut in.

When he typed my name, the results popped up almost immediately. "Oh, there it is. Mia Hunter Chase." He looked up at us with a smile. "I am so sorry for the inconvenience. Here is your key card for a one night stay. Room 604. Enjoy."

Before I could reach the key card, Ethan snatched it from the counter. "Thank you."

I walked next to Ethan as we headed to the elevator. I looked around the lobby with a feeling of uneasiness. There was a man with an earpiece sitting at the bar, he glanced briefly in my direction then looked away. He spoke into his cup of scotch, clearly talking to somebody through an earpiece.

I scanned the lobby to see if anyone would respond. I spotted another man moving his lips as he read the newspaper on the couch by the window, he also had an earpiece.

Ethan pressed the button for the elevator, and I leaned against the wall. "Why are there field agents here?" I asked, trying not to move my lips.

"Precaution," Ethan said. "In case you try to run."

The elevator door opened and Ethan pushed me inside. I stumbled forward and banged against the wall.

Once Ethan stepped inside, I grabbed him by the collar of his shirt and pinned him to the wall. "I really do love you, but you keep tossing me around like an old backpack, and I will break your wrist."

Ethan dropped the bag on the floor and threw his hands up with an alright-fine expression. He leaned into me but only to press the button for the sixth floor.

It took everything I had to let go of his shirt. "What's their game, anyway?" I asked, refocusing my attention.

"Who?"

"The Order."

"It's not my job to know."

His loyalty was admirable but severely misplaced. "If my mother wanted them to have her research, she would have given it to them."

"I'm surprised you're still sticking up for her even after what she did."

I turned to look at him, curiosity eating me up inside. "What did she do?"

"The reason your mother didn't give her research to the Order," Ethan said like it was public knowledge. "She wanted to sell it, and the amount she requested was outrageous. When Warren refused to pay, she took off and destroyed everything."

"What?" I breathed, my heart squeezing in my chest. "That's not true."

Ethan stared at the elevator door. "You didn't know your mother. Just like you didn't know about her affair with Hemsworth."

"Don't." I could feel my hands clutching into fists. "Don't you dare tarnish her name."

He finally turned to look at me. "Do you really think a man like Hemsworth would've gone through all that, had there been nothing between them?"

The elevator pinged and Ethan picked up his bag. The door opened, and he stepped out. I dragged my feet as I followed behind him.

"Stay quiet," Ethan said, inserting the card into the door. "And follow my lead."

The door opened, and we walked into the room. Ethan dropped his bag by the sofa but then froze. I followed his gaze to the king-size bed across the room. My stomach fluttered at the thought of being in the same bed together. I looked at him, wondering how he felt about it but he shook himself off his trance and walked to the window.

"I don't get it. Why hire the Order for this job?" I asked, lying on the sofa. "I mean, being the VP, I'm sure Conor could find better security in a heartbeat."

"The Order offered," Ethan said, opening the blinds. "It's all part of the plan to expose Conor and put an end to his manipulation."

I propped my legs up on the sofa and put an arm over my eyes.

"What are you doing?" Ethan asked.

"What does it look like I'm doing?"

Ethan grunted and fell to his knees, holding his head in his hands. He pressed his eyes shut and stopped breathing as the pain ran its course. I hurried to his side. I wasn't sure what to say, so I just put a hand on his shoulder.

"I'm fine," he said, pushing my hand away.

I pulled back. "Geez, just trying to help," I said, making my way back to the sofa.

Ethan let out an exhausted sigh. "I'm sorry," he grumbled. "It's just that...I don't feel this with anyone but you."

"Does it at least come with a memory?" I asked, but he didn't respond.

We were silent for a long while, then Ethan sat on the floor and supported his arms on his bended knees. "I'm sorry for what I said about your mom and Hemsworth. It wasn't my place."

"That's alright." I slouched on the sofa, my heart weighing like an anvil in my chest. "I rather know the truth than believe a lie, even if it hurts. You should try it."

"Are you hungry?" he asked, brushing me off. "I'm starving."

"What about the bag?"

Ethan shrugged. "We don't have to be here when they come for it."

"Who's coming for it?"

"I don't know."

"Of course, you don't." I rolled my eyes. "What's in it?"

When he didn't respond, I jumped to my feet. "Please don't tell me you've been carrying around a bag without even knowing what's in it?"

He gave me the it's-not-my-job-to-know look, and I

wanted to punch him. "What if there are body parts in there?"

"I think you watch too much TV."

I reached for the zipper, but Ethan pulled the bag away from me. "Don't."

"You're not at all curious to know what's in there?" I asked.

"No."

"Well, I am." As I reached for the bag again, he grabbed my arm and pulled me into him.

I looked into his soft blue eyes, our lips inches apart. I opened my mouth to speak but he was so close, I couldn't think straight. "You're starting to remember us, aren't you? Is that why you're worried about me?"

His eyes dropped to my lips. He swallowed hard as though pushing down the words he really wanted to say. I touched his arm, and his strong muscles hardened. I traced my finger over his chest. He loosened his grip on my arm then caressed his thumb on my skin. My breath quickened at his touch.

"There's something I want to show you," he said, his voice barely above a whisper. I looked up to meet his eyes. He reached to touch my face, and I pressed my cheek into his warm palm.

"Show it to me here," I said.

"I can't…" he breathed. "It's…someone."

Ethan drove us about two hours across the state line to Arizona. He parked in front of a cafe shop then we walked down the street, stopping in front of a gallery.

"What's this?" I asked.

"Let's go inside and see." Ethan pulled the door open for me, and we walked in together.

The place was elegant but modern. The vinyl floor was a dark shade of gray. The paintings on the wall were terrific, the details so well thought out. I walked up to an art that was on display in the corner. It was of a little girl in a ponytail, throwing a glass bottle against a graffiti wall.

"That's my husband's favorite," a woman's voice snuck up behind us. "He had a dream one night and just had to paint it."

I turned around to a redhead with long legs and beautiful curves. "Bonnie?"

Our eyes locked and her jaw dropped open. "Mia?"

I looked around for Ethan, but he had turned his back to us and was standing in front of another painting a few feet away.

"What are you doing here?" Bonnie asked. "I mean, how did you—"

"Hey babe," a man's voice came from the back of the gallery, and my whole body froze as he stepped into view. "The shipment is in—Oh, I'm sorry. I didn't know we had customers."

I stopped breathing. Ethan came to stand next to me, and I clung to his arm, holding back tears.

It was my brother. My beautiful raggedy brother, with his hair just as lengthy as I remembered.

"Honey…" Bonnie reached for Shawn's hand, nervously. "This is actually—"

"An old friend of Bonnie's from school," I cut in, quickly. "Just came to say hi."

Bonnie looked at me, confused.

"Oh, okay." Shawn flashed a smile and tears filled my eyes. "Small world, huh? Well, I'll leave you girls to catch up, then?"

"Do you need any help?" Ethan offered. "You said something about a shipment?"

"That'd be great, thanks."

The boys disappeared from view, but my heart was still aching.

Bonnie turned to me. "What's going on? Why didn't you want your brother to know about you?"

"I'm involved with NeuroCorp."

Bonnie gasped.

"I know," I sighed. "Long story, and I don't want to get him involved. Not again."

She nodded. "Right, of course."

"So, how did you both...?" I wasn't even sure how to even phrase the question. "You're married?"

"Yeah, I know." Bonnie led me to a sofa in the corner then headed to the mini-fridge on the counter. "Would you like some water?"

"Sure."

"So, Hemsworth contacted me out of the blue," Bonnie said, searching through the fridge. "He said Shawn had lost his memory and needed help."

"What kind of help?" I asked.

"I was working for home care, and Hemsworth paid me to nurse Shawn back to health. Mind you, Shawn had just gotten out of a coma. It wasn't easy. He needed help in a lot of things; eating, bathing, you name it." She shook her head. "I still don't know why he came to me, though. It's not like he knew about our history."

Hemsworth did know. He had Shawn's memories. But I didn't bother telling her that. "How did he even find you?" I asked.

"I have no idea, but I wasn't surprised." She handed me the bottled water then sat on the arm of the sofa. "When my brother took me to them years ago, and they found out I was pregnant, they gave me a new identity and helped me disappear from the map."

"Hemsworth did that?"

"Well, not directly. It was some guy named Collins Sr. He talked to Hemsworth and got his approval to give me a new identity and a place to stay here in Arizona."

"Did you know what the procedure was?" I asked.

"Gavin said it was gonna be an ultrasound to make sure the baby was okay, but Mr. Collins told me the truth. He was the one who suggested I stay away from my brother."

"Wow." I took a swig of water to soothe my dry throat. "And all those years Shawn thought you left him."

She sighed. "I know. It broke my heart." She put a hand over her chest. "I can't even count how many times I thought about reaching out to him. But I was so afraid of Gavin finding out where I was and harming the baby."

"I knew your brother hated Shawn, but I had no idea it was that much."

"He always blamed your family for what happened to ours," Bonnie said, drinking her water. "Our dad worked for NeuroCorp, too. He actually worked with your mom."

"Yeah, I know. My mom fired him, right?"

Bonnie nodded.

"I'm sorry about that."

"Oh, don't be." She waved it off. "My dad was sexually

abusing the women nurses and putting them through that procedure for them to forget everything. When your mom found out, she was furious! That's why she fired him."

I couldn't remember ever seeing a female nurse involved with the Catalyst trial. Maybe that was the reason. Maybe my mother didn't hire women anymore after that.

"How do you know all that?" I asked.

"Hemsworth told me," she said. "I didn't want to believe it at first, but then I started to piece together things my mom was saying that night, and I do remember her asking him how many women he took advantage of…" she trailed off, staring blindly at a crack on the wall. "I went to the police station and looked into my father's file. Turns out he was in the sex offenders list. After I saw that, everything started making sense."

I stared at her with eyes full of tears. "I am so sorry you went through all of that."

"Yeah, well…" She looked down and started peeling the label off the bottle. "It's life."

I leaned forward and touched her hand. "I'm glad to see you're happy now," I said, offering a smile.

She smiled back. "I am, and we have two beautiful boys. Shawn Jr. is ten, and little Cole is not even one."

"You have two kids?"

She nodded, grinning from ear to ear. "They're so much like your brother."

"Does he know about Shawn Jr.?"

"He does, but I didn't get into the details about Neuro-Corp," she said. "I did tell him we dated in high school and that I got pregnant. We had a paternity test done, then left it at that."

Typical Shawn, still didn't care to confront things. "Why didn't you tell him? Years ago, I mean."

"I tried, but your brother wasn't ready for kids, and I didn't want to force him into it. Then, as the years went on, it became more and more difficult. After a while, I thought he would just be angry with me for keeping it from him."

There was a loud crash in the back of the gallery, and we both turned to look. "Honey?" Bonnie called out. "Is everything okay?"

"Uh...not sure," Shawn replied. "Can you get your friend in here?"

We jumped up and hurried to the back. Ethan was sitting on the floor, leaning on his bended knees with his back against the wall. He was supporting his head on his hands.

Shawn looked at me, confused. "I just said that was a cool tattoo."

I crouched at Ethan's side and put a hand on his shoulder. I could tell by his relaxed demeanor that the surge had already run its course, and it probably came with a memory of Shawn.

"Come on, honey." Bonnie tugged on Shawn's arm. "Let's give them some privacy."

Once they walked out, Ethan looked up and let out an exhausted breath. "He tattooed our rings, didn't he?"

I ran my fingers through his soft hair. "You remembered."

He lowered his head, pressing his lips together. "What does it mean?" he asked, looking at it.

"Lovers matched by God," I said, caressing the back of his neck. "You picked it out."

"What's wrong?" a child's voice came from behind me. I turned around only to find a young version of my brother, staring at us with big hazel eyes. Wow, he looked just like Shawn, except with a decent haircut.

"He just has a headache," I said to...my nephew.

"Does he want some medicine?" he asked.

"I'm fine." Ethan shrugged it off and pushed himself up. "Thanks anyway, kid."

"Shawny, get over here," Bonnie called in a hushed tone. "Leave them alone."

"It's okay," I said, turning to her. "Oh, my goodness." She was holding little Cole. He was so adorable with his thin blonde hair glistering under the light.

Bonnie smiled. "The nanny just left for her lunch break," she said. "Wanna hold him?"

"Really?"

She plopped him in my arms, and he squealed, shoving his entire hand into his mouth.

"Wow," Ethan looked over my shoulder. "That is a gift, kiddo."

Cole looked up at Ethan and laughed, removing his little hand from his mouth.

"What's that?" I asked little Cole. "You wanna give uncle Ethan a high-five?"

Ethan stepped back, his face twisting in disgust. "Not with that slobbered hand, you won't."

Cole laughed again, and the high pitched sound lifted my heart from all the worries. I hadn't felt that light in a long time.

Shawn swung an arm around Bonnie's shoulder with a pleased smile. "I think the baby likes your friends."

Bonnie smiled. "Yeah... they're like family."

* * *

BY THE TIME we finished lunch, the nanny had come back and taken the kids into the playroom. Shawn and Bonnie had a loft above the gallery, which made me laugh. So much had changed, yet so much was still the same. Bonnie stood and started cleaning up the table.

"Here," I said, taking some of the plates from her hand. "I'll help you."

I followed her into the kitchen while the boys stayed at the table talking about basketball and drinking beer. She placed the dishes inside the sink and started washing each one by hand.

"So... you and Ethan, huh?" she asked, keeping her voice low. "How did that happen?"

I smiled, my cheeks flushing as I remembered our first kiss. When I tricked Ethan into giving me back the keys. Then, our second kiss when he drenched me in Guinness. "I guess, being roommates got us closer," I said, quietly.

"No kidding." She laughed. "I'm thrilled he found a nice girl. He's always been so precious. I mean, the heart of gold."

I glanced at Ethan and caught him staring at me. He quickly looked away and gulped down what was left of his beer. I couldn't help but smile.

"He sure is," I said under my breath. "He sure is."

We stayed for a little while longer but then it was time to go. Shawn and Bonnie walked us downstairs then out the door. Ethan leaned in to give Bonnie a friendly hug, leaving me standing in front of Shawn.

"It was nice meeting you, Mia." Shawn leaned in for a hug, and when his arms wrapped around me, I squeezed him.

"The pleasure was all mine," I said, pulling back.

"Feel free to come by anytime," he said, smiling. "The gallery is always open."

I nodded, feeling the tears pushing through to the surface. I gave Bonnie one last hug and whispered in her ear, "Take care of my brother for me."

"I will," she whispered back. "Now, be sure to take care of yourself, okay?"

I nodded, though little did she know that the Order had me on strings like a puppet. For all I knew, that was the last time I would ever see them both.

The walk back to the car was silent. Ethan didn't speak, and neither did I—although there was plenty of chatter around us from people walking past. When we finally reached the car, Ethan opened the passenger door for me.

"How did it feel seeing your brother, again?" he asked, sounding genuinely curious.

I pushed myself into him and broke down crying. His strong arms wrapped around me and I buried my face into his warm neck.

"I'm sorry," he whispered, confused. "I thought you would be happy."

"I am," I said, pulling back and wiping my face. "It's just that...how did you know?"

"After Hemsworth died, I was assigned to look into his personal affairs," Ethan explained. "The Order wanted to be sure he wasn't hiding anything else from them." Ethan crossed his arms and leaned against the car. "I noticed he'd been calling this gallery a lot, as well as purchasing quite a few paintings here. I got curious."

"But how did you know Shawn was my brother?" I asked.

"I looked into you," he confessed. "From the moment you were born to the day you were caught. I looked up everything."

I stared at him, speechless.

"What? You were claiming to be my wife." He shrugged. "I had to know the truth."

"And...?"

"And...it's getting late." Ethan pulled the door open. "We should get back to the hotel."

CHAPTER 13

*A*T THE HOTEL, we pulled up under the portico. A black limo was pulling out just as we parked. A valet came with a polite smile to stand outside Ethan's door. We jumped out of the jeep and skipped up the steps.

I scanned around as we crossed the lobby. Ethan didn't seem worried, as if it didn't matter that we were being watched. What bothered me most though, was not knowing who was watching. Field agents didn't usually disguise themselves.

The elevator ride was silent just as the car ride had been. Ethan didn't seem to mind, and I wondered if that was a good thing. Maybe I should have been trying harder to jog his memory of us—of the drive.

When we reached our floor, Ethan shoved his hand into his pocket. He stopped then patted his back pockets.

"What's wrong?" I asked.

"The key card must've fallen in the car," he said, letting out a frustrated sigh. "I'll be right back."

I sat on the floor and leaned back against the wall. Once

the elevator door closed, I stood and pulled out the card key from my pocket. I had taken from Ethan when I leaned into him, crying. If he didn't want to know what was in that bag, that was his choice.

I opened the door but stopped at the sight of Conor in a slim black suit looking out the window. He turned around, his dirty blonde hair reflecting in the late afternoon sun.

"Why hello," he smiled, shoving his hands in his pocket. "What a nice surprise."

I slipped the key card into the door slot and stepped inside, letting the door shut behind me. The bag was empty on the floor, but something that looked like a tripod was set-up by the window.

"What's that?" I asked, pointing to the tripod next to him.

"What, this?" Conor looked at it with a small shrug. "There will be cameras in all of the rooms on the south side so my men can keep an eye out for any unusual activity."

His men? I knew the security downstairs weren't field agents.

"Seeing you here is quite an unusual activity in itself," I said, approaching to get a better look at the tripod. "I would think you have people for that."

"I like to oversee certain things myself," he said. "It's so hard to trust anyone these days."

"Trust issues..." I sighed, reaching for the stand. "I can relate."

"It's Mia, right?" Conor moved closer, tugging at his belt. "I heard good things about you."

"Like what?"

He touched his chest to my back and leaned into my ear. "Like you're not the type to disappoint," he whispered with a flirtatious tone.

"That would certainly depend on your expectation," I murmured back.

"As long as things are done my way, I'm very easy to please," he said, twirling the ends of my hair around his thin fingers.

"A bit of a control freak, I see."

He smiled as he took his time tucking a strand of hair behind my ear. "I'm a freak in more ways than one, actually."

I tried not to cringe. "Are you the type to disappoint?"

He smiled, running the tips of his finger up and down my arm. "I guess you could make your own assessment," he whispered, leaning closer.

"I already have."

He turned me around to face him. "Is that right?" His lips were inches from mine, his breath smelled like coffee. "And what is your evaluation?"

"If you were as good as you claim," I said, unbuttoning his suit jacket. "Then why make those women forget about you?"

Conor looked surprised but then smiled. "Wow… pretty and smart." He licked his lips. "I like it."

I slid my hands into his jacket, and while pushing it off of his shoulders, I leaned into his ear. "Then how about you take my number?"

Conor's lips twisted into a crooked smile as his jacket fell on the floor. He pulled out his phone and handed it to me. Once I typed in the number and saved it, I handed it back to him.

"Why wait?" he asked, pulling me into him, his hands sliding up my back. He bit his lips as he pressed himself onto me. Everything about him was charming, no wonder he'd taken advantage of so many women.

He tried kissing my lips, but I turned away. He nibbled on my neck, and I was surprised at how good that actually felt, but only because I hadn't been touched by a man in far too long. I definitely underestimated my hormones when I decided to lead him on.

The door swung open, and he stopped. Ethan was staring at us with his jaw tightened and his fists clenched into a ball, the veins in his forearm about to burst.

Conor chuckled. "Your bodyguard's here," he muttered as he pulled back. He picked up his suit jacket from the floor then slipped it on. "Nice chatting with you." He flashed a devious smile. "See you around."

Once Conor left, Ethan slammed the door behind him. I tried escaping into the bathroom, but Ethan caught me and pinned me against the threshold.

"Why would you let a man like that touch you?" he hissed.

I looked up to meet his eyes. "Somebody's got to."

Suddenly, his lips were on mine. I gasped as he found my tongue, he tasted like spearmint. He pressed his strong body onto me, still pinning me against the threshold. I grabbed two fists full of his hair and pulled him into me. He lifted me off the ground, and I wrapped my legs around his waist. Within a second, his shirt was gone and so was mine. He laid me on the bed, his body heavy on top of me.

"Oh, God..." I moaned. "I need you to stop."

"Why?" he breathed.

"Conor will be back."

At hearing Conor's name, Ethan pulled back.

"I know..." I breathed, struggling to find enough self-control to keep from ripping the rest of Ethan's clothes.

"Why is he coming back here?"

I pushed Ethan off of me. "I don't have time to explain," I said, pulling out of my pocket Conor's cell phone.

"You took his phone?"

"Yes, from his jacket when he was...distracted."

"That's why you let him kiss you?"

"Of course." I rolled my eyes like that should've been obvious. "I'm lonely Ethan, not desperate."

"Well, dumb move. You don't have his code."

"Actually, I do." I flashed him a cunning smile. "I saw it when he took my number."

I quickly opened the messages and scanned through them. There were so many, I wasn't even sure what I was looking for.

Ethan looked toward the door. "Someone's coming." He stood and put his ear against the door. "Hurry up."

I opened a new message. "I need more time," I said, typing in Rashida's number as fast as I could. VP's phone. Don't reply. Hack it.

"There is no time," Ethan said in a hushed tone.

There was a knock on the door and Ethan reached for our shirts on the floor. I deleted the message just as he snatched the phone from my hand. He threw it on the ground and pulled me into the closet with him, closing it only halfway to give the illusion that it was empty.

There was another knock on the door, and we crouched as far into the closet as we could. The sound of the key card sliding through the slot echoed in the small room, and the door swung open. Conor walked in with two guards following behind. He glanced around and let out a breath of relief when he saw his phone by the foot of the bed. He picked it up and turned to face the guards.

"Sir?" They stood in front of Conor as if waiting for further instructions.

"Nothing, false alarm." Conor waved it off. "Go make sure everything is set in the other rooms."

"Yes, sir."

Once the guards left, a man with black hair and leather jacket walked in. "It's about time," Conor complained, closing the door behind him.

"I was busy," the man said with a strange sense of authority. "But I'm here now, so what's the deal?"

"The deal?" Conor leaned into the leather jacket man. "Let's get something straight...you work on my schedule, understood?"

The man nodded, though unfazed. "Yes, sir."

Conor walked to the window, and the man followed. "This is it, can you make the shot from here?"

"Please, don't offend me." The man in the leather jacket bent down and grabbed the tripod as though a sniper gun was resting on it. I held back a gasp, and Ethan put a hand over my mouth.

"This will be no problem," the man said, pulling away from the window. "The president won't even see it coming."

"Good," Conor said pulling out his phone and looking

down at the screen. "I have a meeting to get to. Go out back and dodge the cameras."

Once Conor walked out, and the man followed, I stumbled out of the closet and hurried to the window.

"Conor is planning to assassinate the president?" I echoed, slipping my shirt back on. "Did you know about this?"

Ethan put his shirt on then took a seat on the edge of the bed. "Yes and no."

I looked at him, horrified. "What does that even mean?"

"I was the one hired to take that shot," he admitted.

"You were hired to kill the president?"

"No..." Ethan looked up at me. "I was hired to kill Conor."

I leaned back against the window, confused.

"Conor thinks we're here to shoot the president," Ethan explained. "But we're here to shoot him."

"Clearly, you're not the only sniper he hired."

"And that presents a problem."

"Ya think?" I stared at Ethan, baffled. "Your prints are all over that bag. My name is on the reservation for this room. We're not here to help. We're here to take the blame for everything."

Ethan pulled out his phone. "You're paranoid."

"Am I?"

Though he looked down at his screen, I could tell he was listening because he didn't dial anything.

"We need to leave now," I said, heading toward the door. "And call Warren. Tell him to meet us at the compound."

CHAPTER 14

AS SOON AS we walked into the control room, I pulled Ethan's gun from his belt and pointed at Warren's back. He swung the executive chair around, unfazed.

"Please, put the gun down," he said calmly.

"It was a trap, wasn't it?" I hissed. "Wasn't it?"

"Yes, it was." He laced his fingers together and leaned back. "But it was all part of the plan."

"What plan?" I clutched to the gun tighter. "Tell me everything or I'll shoot you."

"Fine." Warren stood, and I stepped back, keeping the gun aimed at him. He shoved his hands into his pockets and started pacing. "Once Conor's killed, you will take the blame. So naturally, the president will send out a hunt for you. And when he finds out we have you, he won't be able to resist agreeing to an audience with us." Warren stopped and turned to me. "Once we finally get him in the same room, we will tell him everything Conor has done concerning the Catalyst trial—including all the women he's abused. Of course, it will be made to believe that you were one of those women and that's why you shot him." Warren's lips lifted into a pleased smile. "After we give him the list of all the women under the white house roof that has been a victim of Conor's, the president will have no choice but to pardon you."

"Why didn't you just tell me I was the scapegoat?"

"Think of it as a Trojan Horse," Warren said. "Now please, put that gun away."

I lowered the gun and allowed Ethan to take it from me. "Well, Conor seems to be arranging his own backup plan."

"What?" Warren looked at Ethan. "What is she talking about?"

"It's true," Ethan confirmed, shoving his gun back onto his belt. "He has another sniper in place."

Warren cursed under his breath as he leaned forward on the oval table. "Someone must've tipped him off."

"Do you think it might've been Sadykov?" Ethan asked.

Warren rubbed his chin with a thoughtful gaze. "That's exactly what I was thinking. Alright, here's what we're gonna do. They have no idea that we know their plan, so that means we are one step ahead of them. Ethan, you are gonna find a way to sabotage that sniper, and you..." He looked at me with boldness in his eyes. "Brace yourself for what's coming."

* * *

While in the shower, I closed my eyes under the hot water and took a deep relaxing breath as the warmth soothed what was left of my scars.

"Are you crazy?" a squeaky voice came from behind me in a hushed tone, and I jumped back, startled.

"Matt?" I tried covering myself with my hands and arms, but it wasn't enough. I pulled the towel that was hanging on top of the stall and wrapped it around me. "Are you out of your mind?"

He grabbed me by my arms and pinned me to the wall. "I came to ask you the same thing," he hissed. "You're helping the Order?"

"How did you…?"

"You can't trust them."

"Matt, I know what I'm doing."

"No, you don't understand. The opposition won't be able to fight against you—"

"The opposition?"

"Mia, we have to leave this place. Come with me, and we'll run away tonight."

"I already told you, I'm not leaving Ethan."

He pressed me harder against the wall. "Ethan is gone. I know you're hoping that everything is going to work out just fine, but it won't. Not this time—"

"What did you say?"

"Run away with me."

"No, before that." I studied him, carefully. "You said, everything is going to work out just fine."

"Yeah, so?"

I grabbed his wrist and twisted to his back then pinned his face against the stall. He held back a scream, but I didn't care.

"That's something the old Ethan would say," I hissed into his ear. "You have his memories, don't you?" I twisted his wrist even more, and he squirmed. "Don't you?"

"Yes!"

I grabbed his hair and yanked it back. "Why didn't you tell me?"

He winced as his body bent out of shape. "I was afraid you would take it from me."

"It doesn't belong to you." I let Matt go and stepped back. "You were never with Rashida and the crew, were you?"

He turned around, massaging his wrist. "No."

I paced around the small space, trying to process everything. When he took a step toward me, I put my hand on his chest. "Don't."

"I'm sorry, I lied to you." There was sadness in his eyes. "No, I was never part of the opposition. But once I got Ethan's memories and understood your side of the story, I changed. I switched sides."

I shook my head. "You shouldn't have kept it from me."

"Mia, please. Don't help them—"

I pressed the palm of my hand over Matt's mouth and pushed him down. The sound of footsteps was drawing closer.

"We can't do this here," I whispered. "Meet me in the woods behind the medical wing at midnight."

The bathroom door swung open. "Who are you talking to?" Ethan asked.

I stood from the floor and turned off the water. "Nobody," I said, stepping out. "The towel got wet, and now I'm freezing."

When I noticed him trying to look over my shoulder, I

dropped the towel. His eyes widened, and he turned around.

"Can I have a dry towel, please?" Though I couldn't see his face, I could hear him swallowing hard. "You're surprisingly respectful for a cold-blooded killer, by the way."

When he didn't respond, I could tell even his own reaction had taken him by surprise. He took a deep breath before reaching for another towel inside the cabinet.

"Do you really think they'll come through for me?" I asked, wrapping myself around the dry towel.

"Yes." Ethan finally turned around to look at me. "Once they get the president to listen, everything will be fine."

"What if he doesn't listen?"

"He will."

"How can you be so sure?"

"Because I'll make sure to release a report that you were abused by Conor," Ethan explained. "After that, I'm sure quite a few women will report the same."

"That would be a lie, though."

"Not really." Ethan shrugged. "Just think of how many women you'll be helping. It really did happen to them."

"What if those women don't remember?"

"We have footage of every single one of them making a statement before their so-called physical. I'm sure proving won't be a problem." Ethan took a step closer, and my heart began to race. "We're on the same team here, Mia."

"Except, I'm the scapegoat."

Ethan held my face with his warm hands. "I'm not gonna let anything happen to you."

The door squeaked, and I grabbed Ethan's face and

kissed him before he could turn around and see Matt sneaking out.

I was caught by surprise when Ethan tightened his arms around me and lifted me off the ground. By the time he pushed me back into the stall, his kiss had deepened. My heart drummed so hard I thought for sure he could hear it. He pinned me to the wall, and my head started to spin.

A loud thud hit the door, and Ethan ripped himself off of me. He turned toward the door, alarmed. "What was that?" he asked, out of breath.

Matt, for sure. I was going to murder him. "No idea."

Ethan stepped back. "I'm gonna go check," he said, taking a deep breath. "You, get dressed."

And just like that, I was alone again.

* * *

WHEN THE CLOCK HIT MIDNIGHT, I jumped out of bed and left my room, using Matt's access card. As soon as I stepped outside, the freezing cold stiffened every bone in my body. I started to run, trying to warm up, though still careful not to call any attention. I crossed the empty courtyard then ducked behind a tree as two armed field agents appeared.

They talked in hushed tones as they walked past and I pressed my back against the trunk, trying hard to keep still. Once they entered the building I'd exited from, I rushed to the building behind.

I scanned Matt's card at every door until I finally arrived at the control room. I peeked inside and saw two agents sitting across from each other. Though they were sitting in front of the monitors, their eyes were on each other's hands as they held up their cards on top of the table.

I kicked the door and ran around the bend. I hid behind the wall and listened for them. I heard footsteps and pulled out the taser I had also taken from Matt. As soon as one of the agents walked past me, I grabbed him from behind and shocked him on his back. His body shuddered then his legs went limp. It took all of my strength to hold him up on his feet. I leaned my back against the wall for support and listened for the other pair of footsteps.

Once the other agent came around the corridor, I charged in his direction using his friend's body as a shield and shocked him on his rib cage. A painful growl ripped through his throat as his body trembled out of control. When he dropped to the floor, I threw the first agent on top of the second and shocked them both, again. Just in case.

After making sure they were both knocked out, I ran into the control room, which they'd left opened, and rushed to the computer. I crouched underneath the control panel and followed the thick black wire all the way to the external drive. I yanked out the mid-size black box, as well as the cable for the security cameras. Once everything was disconnected, I rushed to exit the building.

Matt was leaning against a tree, and his face lit up when he saw me.

"Here." I grabbed his backpack from the ground and shoved the external drive inside. "Take this."

"What's that?" he asked.

"The external drive from the control room," I said. "It

may not have everything we need, but there's gotta be something we can use."

"We don't need that," Matt said, pulling a flash drive out of his pocket. "I got the drive Ethan took from Fort Benning."

"Wait, I thought Ethan injected himself with a serum that made him forget where he hid the drive?"

"That's what I told them."

"Matt..." I grabbed his face and kissed him on the forehead. "You're a genius!"

Matt smiled, blushing.

"I'll keep this," I said, taking the flash drive from his hand, "but take the external drive to Rashida. She'll know what to do with it."

"Wait..." His smile faded when he noticed I wasn't going with him. "You're not coming?"

"I can't," I said. "My job here isn't done."

"Ethan will never pick you over them," Matt insisted. "Mia, listen to me—"

I shoved a piece of paper inside his pocket, ignoring him. "Call this number and Rashida will find you."

"How?" he asked. "Are you sure?"

"Positive. Now get moving!" I pushed his backpack into his chest. "You have to get as far away from here as possible."

"So do you." Matt grabbed my arm and looked me in the eyes. "Once they see that the external drive is gone, they will come after you."

"They won't because I used your access card." I touched his shoulder. "It's fine. They think I'm on their side."

Matt nodded but made no effort to move. The crackling of leaves echoed in the distance, and we both turned around, frightened.

"Go, Matt!" I whispered. "And do not come back for me. I'll get out of here as soon as the time is right."

Matt wrapped me in a tight embrace that lasted longer than he could afford then finally started to run, disappearing into the darkened woods.

* * *

I walked outside just as the sun was rising. I tried soaking up as much of the warmth of the sun as I could, but the wind was just brutal.

As I strolled across the courtyard, I was surprised to see so many soldiers already up. Some groups were drenched in sweat as if they'd been training for hours. One soldier, in particular, seemed to be struggling with a box he was carrying. He placed it on the ground to catch his breath.

"Hey," he called out to me. "Can you help me carry this over there?"

I glanced behind me to make sure he was really talking to me.

He laughed. "Yes, you."

"Oh, sure." I crouched on the other side of the box and waited for him to lift his side. "Whenever you're ready."

He leaned down, and we lifted the box together. It wasn't as heavy as I thought it would be, but I didn't question it. He walked backward, leading the way as I followed.

"Okay. We don't have much time," he said quickly, trying not to move his lips. "My name is Seth. I'm a friend of Hugh's. He's been informing me of what the Order has been doing to the soldiers and I, for my part, have been informing my team. I've been discreet, and I know who to tell. As of now, I have quite a few assembled and ready whenever you all need. Please, let Hugh know that since I have lost contact with him."

"When did you last hear from him?" I asked.

"Last week. Tell him I am no longer in Fort Knox, but not to worry. I've transferred my unit here, and we're counting on getting a lot more." He stopped next to a utility room outside the building and signaled for me to put the box down. After we lowered the box together, he stepped back and saluted me. "Thank you for your help."

"No problem." I waved it off. "Have you seen Ethan?"

"Yes, he's training at the PT Center."

***

THE PT CENTER was about a mile stretch of sand under various obstacles that were typically used in phase three of their military training. Climbing walls and crawling in the mud was just some, among the many. Stage four was similar, but instead of a flat surface, it was at the side of a mountain.

Ethan was already making his way back by the time I arrived. I sat on a bench and watched him. He was covered in mud, even on his face. He jumped and swung and crawled so effortlessly, I could see why the Order found him so valuable.

When he climbed the last wall, he fell to his feet and paced around the sand, taking deep, steady breaths. He pulled off his shirt to wipe his face and the sight of his strained muscles knocked the air out of me. He squirted water on his hair as well as his mouth, and as the clear liquid slid down his upper body, I couldn't stop thinking of what almost happened at the hotel.

I stood, and leaves broke under my shoes. Ethan turned around, alarmed.

"Sorry." I threw my hands up. "I didn't mean to startle you."

"What are you doing up so early?" he asked, still breathing heavy from of the exertion.

"I needed to see you."

"Why?" He cocked his head, curious. "Mia, what's wrong?"

I reached for his face. "Please, don't fight it. You know I'm telling you the truth. Even if you don't remember everything, I know you can feel it. I know it."

He nodded ever so slightly, and my heart flared with hope.

"Run away with me," I urged, peering into his eyes. "We can leave tonight."

"What about the Catalyst trial—"

"I don't care about that, anymore. I just want to be married and happy and safe with you."

He opened his mouth to speak but stopped when he saw two soldiers marching in our direction.

"Major General, sir!"

Ethan moved away from me. "Yes, soldier?"

"Your presence is being requested in the gray room, sir!"

"I'll be right there."

"Also, the girl needs to come with us, sir," the soldier added. "Mr. Warren has requested to see her."

Ethan looked at me, his eyes full of concern.

"Sir?"

"Right," Ethan nodded. "Take her."

As soon as I entered the control room, Conor raised his hand to stop Warren from talking. Sadykov leaned back on his chair and crossed his arms.

"Mia." Conor stood. "Thank you for coming."

I didn't know I had a choice, but I kept that to myself. I looked at Warren trying to ignore how uneasy Conor made me feel.

"So, we had break-in last night," Conor said, circling around me like a shark. "You wouldn't know anything about that, would you?"

"Should I?" I asked, trying hard to keep my voice steady.

"I think it's time you pick a side." Conor pulled out a gun and held it out to me. "There's a man next door who committed treason. Shoot him."

Warren stood. "Now, is that really necessary?"

Conor glared at him. "Would you prefer I bring your grandkids in here?"

Warren lowered his head and stepped back.

"Now..." Conor turned his attention back to me. "Either you're with us or against us."

"Who is he?"

"That doesn't concern you," Conor said, walking around the table. "But perhaps this could jog your memory?" He threw the external drive on top of the table, and I held back a gasp.

Oh, God. It was Matt.

I gulped, hoping I wouldn't start sweating.

"So, what's it gonna be?" Conor asked, sliding the gun across the table toward me. "Are you with us or against us, Ms. Hunter?"

Sadykov kicked his chair back in a fury. "Answer the question!"

"Fine," I hissed, taking the gun. "I'll do it."

Conor smiled. "Good choice."

The main monitor came into focus, and when I saw the image, my heart nearly shattered in my chest. Matt was tied to a chair with duct tape over his mouth and his arms tied behind his back. A male nurse stepped forward and placed a pillowcase over his head. His body started to shudder, and his muffled screams echoed off the grey walls.

"What did he do?" I asked, struggling to keep my voice from cracking.

"He took something from us," Conor said. "And we caught him trying to contact the opposition."

I stared at the screen, holding back tears. That was all my fault. He was going to die, and it was all my fault.

"Enough with the chit-chat." Conor pulled the door open. "Go prove yourself."

I took a deep breath as I walked to next room. My hands were shaking when I pushed open the door. Two soldiers stood behind me to make sure I followed through. Conor, Warren, and Sadykov stayed in the control room, watching through the glass window. The camera in the corner was flashing red. I gripped the handle of the gun as tight as I could then turned my attention to Matt.

His knees were trembling, and although I couldn't see

his hands because his skinny arms were tied behind the chair, I was almost positive it was shaking, too.

I clicked the gun and Matt started to scream, even though his mouth was taped over. He kept trying hard to rip himself from the metal chair but stopped when I touched the gun to his head. As I was about to pull the trigger, I jerked my elbow into the soldier's stomach. His body bent over, and I rammed my knee into his face. The other soldier charged toward me, but in one swift move I pulled out the taser from the first soldier's belt and shocked the second one on the chest.

After dropping both bodies on the ground, I shoved the gun behind my belt, and I rushed toward Matt. When I pulled off the pillowcase from his head, my whole body froze.

It wasn't Matt.

It was Dale.

"You can still redeem yourself, Hunter," Conor spoke through the intercom. "After all, Dale told us where to find the opposition. We caught them all."

"You're lying," I said, turning toward the glass window. I wish I could see Conor's face, but I was only able to see my own reflection.

"How do you think we caught Matt, sweetheart?" Conor asked, his voice wickedly calm. "You kill the man in front of you, and we won't harm your father, or your sister, or your little brother whose leg still isn't fully healed."

I pointed the gun to Dale's forehead, and he started to cry. He tried to speak through the duct tape, but it was muffled.

He was a traitor, I kept telling myself. My whole family

was in the hands of the Order because of him. They were all most likely being tortured as we speak, and it was all because of him. He deserved to die. I pulled back the hammer, and the gun clicked. Dale closed his eyes and tears slid down his face.

Pull the trigger, Mia. Don't think about it, just pull the trigger.

I couldn't do it. I put the gun down and disarmed it.

Conor sighed through the intercom. "Let me show you what loyalty looks like."

The monitor in the corner turned on, and the image of Matt tied to a chair appeared, again. That image wasn't recorded in that room. Matt wasn't even wearing camo pants. How did I miss that?

"Major general," Conor barked into the intercom, and Ethan stepped forward.

"No..." I held my breath as he raised his gun. "Ethan, no..."

"Kill him."

Ethan pointed the gun to Matt's chest, and without any hesitation, he pulled the trigger.

No! I stormed back to the control room and used Matt's access card to get in. I pointed the gun at Conor's smiling face.

"I knew it." He shook his head. "When I saw Matt's card logged in last night, I knew he couldn't have taken the drive. The poor kid pees his pants for much less, he couldn't possibly have gotten through the guards."

"If you knew he didn't do it, why did you kill him?" I hissed, gripping the gun like I could crush it.

"There are only two options, remember?" He said as

though he'd done nothing wrong. "Either you're with us, or you're against us. He made his choice."

I pulled the trigger right into Conor's chest. Once, twice, three times. But there were no bullets.

Sadykov laughed while Conor ripped the gun from my hand. "Do you really think we would give you a loaded gun?"

I looked at Warren, but he still didn't say anything.

"Oh, Mia." Conor sighed. "I really wish we had been wrong about you. You would've been such a nice addition to the team."

"Now that you failed..." Sadykov hissed, clutching his fits into a ball. "You and I get to continue where we left off."

I stepped back, but three agents stormed into the room and charged toward me. I fought them off as much as I could, but it had been over twenty-four hours since I had any sleep—

Oh, no. The mind lock!

I stopped fighting and allowed the agents to pin me to the wall. When Sadykov came at me with his taser, I closed my eyes and braced myself.

CHAPTER 15

I WOKE UP drenched and shivering. I was sitting on a wooden chair with my hands tied behind my back. I looked around and noticed the gray walls. That was the same room Matt was killed in, but his body was no longer there. There were stains of blood on the floor, but it was dry. Who knows how many innocent people they've killed down there.

Two agents dragged another man into the room and sat him in Matt's chair. He also had a white pillowcase over his head, and his screams too were muffled.

"Is she awake, yet?" Sadykov asked over the intercom. "Wake her up!"

An agent came at me with another bucket of iced water and threw it at my face. My whole body shuddered.

"Dale told us about the mindlock," Sadykov spoke through his clenched teeth. "How do we turn it off?"

Part of me wanted to laugh. Had Sadykov not knocked me out with his taser earlier, he actually would have gotten into my head.

"What do you want from me?" I asked, stuttering from the cold. "I don't have my mother's memory."

"You've seen the full journal," Sadykov replied. "That's all we need for now. And we are gonna get it, whether you cooperate or not."

The soldier dropped the bucket and came at me with his taser, but I kicked it off his hand and trapped his neck around my legs. He tried struggling free, but I pressed harder, cutting off his oxygen. Once he passed out, I let his body drop to the floor.

"Suit yourself," Sadykov said, his voice still coming through the speakers. The door swung open, and Ethan walked in.

Nothing made me panic more than seeing Ethan on their side. "Ethan, don't listen to them!" I tried freeing my hands, but they were too tight. "They are manipulating you. You are not a killer."

He placed a taser on the end of a metal stick and started toward the man on the chair. When he pulled the pillowcase off his face, I couldn't breathe.

"No!"

"Remove the tape from his mouth," Sadykov ordered. "I want her to hear him scream."

"Ethan, don't hurt him!"

Ethan pulled the tape off of my brother's face then shocked him on his side. Shawn's body shuddered violently, and his head was thrown back.

"Ethan, stop!"

"Do it again!" Sadykov ordered.

"Ethan, please..." I cried. "He has a heart condition, please!"

Ethan stared at Shawn, completely frozen. Was he remembering him? God, please remember. Please.

"Ethan, again!" Sadykov barked. "That's an order!"

When Ethan didn't move, I could tell he was torn. I could tell he didn't wanna do it anymore.

"I said again, soldier," Sadykov spoke in full authority.

Ethan snapped out of it and shocked Shawn, again.

"Stop!" I cried. "Ethan, please!"

"You want him to stop?" Sadykov said to me. "Then tell me how to turn off the mindlock."

Ethan shocked Shawn again, and I threw my body backward letting my weight drop on top of the wooden chair. The wood shattered beneath me, and I flipped my tied hands to my chest.

I charged toward Ethan, reaching for his wrist. I twisted it until he lost his grip on the taser. It dropped to the ground, and I kicked it across the room.

"Ace?" Shawn's voice was faint behind me, but it landed on my ears like a thunderstorm. "Is that really you?"

Ethan grunted and jerked back with his hands on his head. His back hit the wall, and I turned to my brother with tears in my eyes.

"You remember me?" I asked, my voice barely above a whisper.

"Shoot him!" Sadykov's voice echoed off the walls, and I froze. Ethan stood, his expression stone cold and his eyes...pitch black.

"Ethan, no!" I charged at him, but he was too quick in raising his gun and pulling the trigger. He fired three shots into Shawn's chest, and it felt as if those bullets pierce through my heart.

"Shawn!" I darted to my brother's side as he was struggling to breathe. I yanked his body free from the chair and lay him gently on the ground. "Oh, God." I tried pushing the heel of my hand onto his wound, but there was too much blood. "Stay with me." I ripped off my sleeve and pressed into his chest. "Stay with me."

"Ace..." Shawn grimaced as he touched the back of my hand. "After you left..." he choked, "Bonnie told me everything. I remember you now."

I put more pressure on his chest, trying to stop the bleeding, but it wasn't working. He was bleeding too much, too fast. "I'm right here. Stay with me."

He opened his eyes and looked at me. "It's okay, Ace." He squeezed my hand as he gasped for air. "It's okay."

"No!" I blinked the tears away, fighting against the tightness in my chest. "I can't lose you again. Oh God, I can't."

Shawn grabbed my wrist. "My family...protect them."

"No..." I started to sob. "Shawn, don't."

"Promise me, Ace." He choked again, and blood splattered out of his mouth.

"I promise." I placed his head on my lap and rocked him back and forth until he took his last breath. "I promise." I buried my face in his neck and drenched his cold skin with my tears. "I promise."

Ethan sat on the floor across from us, with tears in his eyes. He looked just as in shock and heartbroken as Rashida had been after she pushed Victor off the cliff.

The door swung open, and I heard a stampede of footsteps barge into the room. I pulled back and closed my brother's eyes just as a hand grabbed my shoulder. I felt the force of a lightning bolt strike my brain and gripped my brother's arms. "I promise," I whispered one last time. When I glanced at my reflection on the metal chair, my eyes were pitch black.

* * *

I FELT a sting on my neck, and I was no longer in the gray room. I was somewhere else in the facility, surrounded by hundreds of field agents blacked out on the floor.

What had I done?

"Somebody stop her!" Conor yelled.

"I think I got her." Sadykov appeared from behind a desk as my arms began to tingle and my legs to wobble. I pulled a dart out of my neck then my arms went numb. I tried to keep myself on my feet, but I stumbled over the body of an agent.

"Relax," Conor spoke from behind me, but I couldn't turn around. "It was only a third of the serum. You won't go completely numb. After all, you still haven't told us what we want to know."

"Enough!" Warren barked at Conor. "Why are you still here? Don't you have a job to do?"

Conor nodded. "Yes, sir."

Sir?

The room began to spin and my stomach to spasm. I was going to gag. Warren crouched down and grabbed my face. "Do you realize we are going to continue killing every single person you love until we get what we want?"

I spit on his face then bent over and vomited at his feet.

I heard him let out a heavy exhale, then Sadykov pulled me up and pinned me against the wall. He turned my head so that I could see Ethan being tied with a rope across the room.

"Please, don't," I cried as I watched the rope wrap around his neck. "Please."

Warren stood behind Sadykov. "Tell us what we want to know."

When I didn't respond, Warren signaled for one of the agents to pull the rope. Ethan's feet left the ground, and he started to choke.

"Stop!"

"How do we turn off the mind-lock?"

"Stop, please!"

Warren took out his taser and shocked Ethan. His body shuddered in the air, making him choke even more. When his eyes began to roll back, my heart started to bleed.

"Twenty-four hours!" I cried, dropping to my knees as Sadykov loosened his hold on me. "I can't sleep for twenty-four hours. Please... stop hurting him."

Warren signaled for Ethan to be put down. Ethan dropped to the ground coughing, his hands still tied.

"Good job, Lieutenant." Warren nudged Ethan's leg. "You got it out of her. You've just earned a promotion."

Ethan didn't respond.

"You two!" Warren pointed to the agents. "Pick her up."

The agents came and lifted me off the floor. I could barely feel their touch as they dragged me into a room, strapped me to a metal chair, and locked a shock brace around my neck. After injecting me with the mobility serum, they set the metal collar to shock every two minutes to keep me awake.

I searched for Ethan, but he was hiding his eyes from me.

"Watch her," Warren said to the agents. "If she's not in this chair in twenty-four hours. You're all dead, understand?"

"Yes, sir." They responded in unison as they stood, one on each side of me.

Warren stepped in front of me and reached for my face. "See? Now that wasn't so hard, was it?"

* * *

TWENTY-FOUR HOURS CAME AND WENT, and there was nothing I could do to stop it. I sat on the metal chair, wholly defeated, getting shocked every two minutes. My brother's lifeless body was gone, and so was Ethan, and all I was left with were images of Ethan shaking Warren's hand and accepting the promotion. Matt was right, my Ethan was never coming back, and that made me wish he would've been dead all along. My heart ached so much less when he was gone than it did at that moment.

I closed my eyes, unsure of whether or not I still felt the shocks. Either my neck was numb, or I had gone completely delirious. I vaguely heard Sadykov's voice in the intercom. The nurses injected the paralyzing serum before unstrapping me from the chair. Though they wore masks, one of them looked like Dale. They carried me to the Catalyst, and the machine was turned on. The red lights appeared and started to spin like fire.

I closed my eyes again, knowing it wouldn't make a difference. They won. They got my memories...and everything with it.

CHAPTER 16

I WOKE UP entwined in Ethan's warmth. We were lying on a bed in a dark room. Ethan was running his hand up and down my back, and I wondered if I was dreaming.

"What happened?" I whispered, pushing through my dry throat. "Where am I?"

"It's an abandoned cottage I found during my training a few months ago," Ethan whispered back. "We're safe for now."

"How come I still remember?" I asked, looking up to meet his eyes. The moonlight broke through the blinds, bathing the room a silvery glow. "Didn't they take my memory?"

"They did," Ethan said with a defeated sigh. "But Dale snuck in there and changed the settings when he put you in the Catalyst. Although your memory was retracted, it wasn't erased."

"What good will my memories do, anyway?" I asked,

barely able to keep my eyes open. "It's not like I had my mother's memories."

"You saw the missing pages," Ethan explained. "That seemed to be all they needed."

How could I have failed? And saved by Dale, out of all people. "Why would Dale help me?" I asked, skeptically. "He betrayed everyone."

"Dale never gave them up. The opposition is still out there. And he helped you because you spared his life."

A wave of relief washed over me, and I clung to Ethan's warm body.

He squeezed me in his arms. "I am never letting them hurt you, ever again," he whispered.

My heart sank as I felt his strength. "How can I trust you?" I whispered back, knowing I should rip myself away from him. "You accepted a promotion—"

"I had to. That was the only way I could get you out of there."

"You killed Matt in cold blood."

"I killed him because he was going to die, anyway," he explained. "There were two field agents behind me, aiming their guns to his chest. If I didn't shoot him, they would have."

"You should've let them."

"I needed the Order to keep trusting me."

"Why?"

He looked down to meet my eyes. "It was the only way to keep you close." He touched my cheek as though caressing a feather. "I've believed you from day one, Mia. I just didn't want to admit it."

"Why now?"

His eyes filled with tears. "You stood your ground in the face of your brother's death," he said, wincing at the painful memory, "but you crumbled in the face of mine."

When Shawn's image surfaced my mind, I closed my eyes and felt a tear slide down my cheek. He tightened his embrace around me, and I buried my face into his neck.

"I'm not torn, anymore," he whispered. "I may not remember everything, but I feel it with every ounce of my being."

"Feel what?"

"Like I want to make love to you."

I looked up at him. "Then, do it."

He cupped my face in his strong hands, his eyes burning with desire. He rolled atop of me and pressed his lips to mine. He kissed me with all the intensity and passion he'd kept bottled up inside.

After we finally came as one, we laid in silence staring up at the wooden ceiling with only the faint sound of cicadas outside. Our bodies were tired but satisfied as we rested in each other's arms.

I rolled over to face him, and he traced my cheek with his finger. "I love you so much," he breathed.

"Words don't do justice to what I feel for you."

He smiled, still caressing my cheek. "You looked so beautiful in your wedding dress."

"You remember that?"

Before he could respond, his eyes rolled back, and his body began to convulse. I jumped up, wrapping myself on the sheets.

"I'm right here, love." I ran my fingers through his hair,

trying to keep myself calm while the seizure ran its brutal course. "I'm right here."

* * *

IT WAS the longest five minutes of my life. I sat on a wooden chair, fully dressed, and stared at his peaceful face as he slept.

"If she keeps having these surges, she will keep seizing, and that could have a terrible effect on her brain." Rashida's words to Hugh kept echoing in my head. She'd said them when I experienced my first seizure, and for all the four hours that he slept, that's all I could think about.

"Hey…" Ethan opened his eyes. "When did you get dressed?"

I sighed. "I have to go."

"What's wrong?" he asked, sitting up. "What happened?"

"You had a grand mal seizure."

"I did?"

"It was caused by your surges," I explained, trying to keep my voice from cracking. "And it will keep happening for as long as I'm around you."

"How do you know that?" he asked.

"It happened to me, too."

"Okay…" He looked around wondering where to go from here. "How do we fix it?"

"You would need your memories back."

"And how do we get that?"

"We can't," I said with my heart sinking in my chest. "The Order most likely destroyed your disk after giving your memories to Matt."

Ethan rubbed his face. "So, now what?"

"I can't..." My voice cracked, and I stood. "I have to leave."

"Wait, what?" Ethan wrapped a sheet around his waist and followed me to the kitchen. "What are you talking about?"

"Being around me will cause more surges, and if they keep happening, it will damage your brain."

"I don't care—"

"But I do!"

He took a step toward me, but I moved back. "Ethan, don't."

"There must be another way."

"I wouldn't be able to live with myself if anything happened to you." As soon as I said those words, I suddenly understood. "Of course.." I looked at him with a sudden awareness while he looked at me, confused. "That's why you walked away. Why you let me believe we had an affair. Why you let me go back to Hugh."

He looked at me like I was speaking a different language. "When did I walk away?"

When I found out about him and followed him to that motel. He had my file. He'd read about the surges and the seizures. That was why he didn't tell me who he really was, he knew that him being around me would've done more harm than good.

Ethan stared at me, waiting for me to say something. "Mia?"

I shook my head. "You wouldn't remember, but I do. And I understand it now."

"Okay..." he said, trying to make sense of it all. "Why don't we just sit down and I'll get you a cup of water."

"Oh, God." I buried my face in my hands. "This is so hard."

"It doesn't have to be." He tried pulling me into him, but I pushed him away. "Mia, please. Don't do this."

I looked away, unable to bear his gaze. "I won't hurt you, Ethan."

He leaned over the dining table and took a deep breath. He didn't say anything for a long time. Then suddenly, he slapped the bowl of fruit off the table.

I thought about touching his shoulder but decided against it. Feeling his bare skin would only make it harder to let him go.

"I get it," he finally said. "I killed your brother, and now you can't stand to even look at me." He turned around to face me, still holding the sheet to his waist. "I can't blame you."

I felt a knot in my throat and had to bite back the tears. "Ethan, that's not the reason—"

"Take the dirt bike." He reached for the keys and threw it on the table. "It's faster and better on gas."

"Ethan, stop."

He picked up his jacket from the floor and threw it on top of the keys. "Take this, too," he said. "It's freezing out there."

I looked at the jacket but couldn't bear to move. Ethan walked away, shaking his head. I wanted to call out to him and assure him that what happened with Shawn had nothing to do with my decision, but he escaped into the bathroom and slammed the door. The walls shook as the sound echoed through the cabin.

Maybe it was for the best.

CHAPTER 17

*E*THAN HAD CASH inside the pocket of his jacket, so I was able to put gas and grab a bite to eat without stopping for too long. I dialed Rashida's number from a payphone, and it rang until it went to voicemail, but it wasn't her voice that came after the beep. There was a faint sound far away in the background. It ended it too soon, so I called again. I covered my ear and closed my eyes, forcing myself to focus.

Water trickling... Ocean? River? Waterfall?

I shot my eyes open with a wave of excitement running through me. I'd found them.

* * *

I HEADED into the woods with my heart tight in my chest. I rode up the trail that led to the Falls. It was the same trail that Shawn and I took the day of my wedding. My stomach turned at the memories, and I had to bite back the tears. I turned off the bike and leaned it against a tree. I took a deep breath, trying hard not to fall apart.

Not now. Not yet.

I continued on the trail on foot. The walk felt a lot longer than previous times I'd hiked, but I was also drained—physically, mentally, and emotionally.

When my eyes finally caught sight of the waterfall, my heart dropped. I walked to the edge of the water and dropped to my knees. My body jerked forward and began to tremble. The tears burst through my defenses, and I had no more strength to hold it in. I grabbed the ground, wheezing. That waterfall was nothing without Ethan. I gasped for air as I attempted to stand. I leaned against a rock, trying to steady my breathing. I took a wobbly step forward, but something caught my foot. There was a loud snap, and before I could react, I was scooped off the ground by a large net. It swung me back and forth. Footsteps rushed in my direction, and the sound of branches breaking came quicker. I thought about screaming, but no one would hear me. It was too far away from the road.

"M's!"

I grabbed on to the net and pulled to turn myself around. "Victor!" Relief washed over me.

"Hold on!" Victor pulled out a pocket knife then reached for the net. I started laughing and crying at the same time. My hysteria only got worse when I thumped to the ground, and Victor put his arms around me. "It's okay, M's." He rocked me back and forth. "It's okay. You're safe, now."

* * *

INSIDE THE CAVE, Victor had hammered white sheets over holes in the wall to give each person a measure of privacy. I laid inside my designated hole for what felt like hours. As tired as I was, I couldn't sleep.

Victor had brought me Benji's laptop, and I had been going through the files in the flash drive Matt had given me, but there was nothing incriminating the Order. Most of the recent documents had been signed by Rashida and Hemsworth. A few had even been signed off by Hugh. Benji had been noted as the main I.T of the program. As for the old documents, it was all under my mother's oversight. It was never Warren's intention to destroy the drive. He purposely gathered incriminating evidence against everyone except himself. In the event the trial was ever discovered and shut down, he most certainly was planning on bargaining his way out of jail.

The sheet moved, and I quickly pulled the drive out of the laptop and shoved it inside my pocket.

"Sorry." Dad raised a hand. "I didn't mean to scare you."

I let out a breath, forcing myself to relax. "It's okay. I've just gotten a bit paranoid."

"Can't blame you." He walked in holding a candle and sat on the floor across from me. The hole was big enough for three people, so we weren't too close. "How are you doing?" he asked.

"I don't know." I rubbed my eyes, fighting a headache. "Sometimes I feel like I'm just hanging by a thread."

He leaned forward, though unsure how to comfort me. "I'm here if you need...anything."

I looked up to meet his eyes, his expression soft in the candlelight. "I'm sorry, Dad."

He looked at me, confused. "About?"

"I thought you had abused Shawn." My voice cracked at the sound of my brother's name, and I pressed my eyes shut to keep the tears at bay. "I spent my whole life hating you for something you never did. That was unfair, and I'm so sorry."

He reached for my hand. "It's okay. I wasn't the father you kids needed, anyway. I neglected you both because I was weak and couldn't handle it. I was selfish, and that was my fault."

"It wasn't your fault, Dad." I opened my eyes and looked at him. "Hemsworth took your memory, leaving you with two kids you couldn't remember having. On top of that, you were told Mom had left you for another man." I shook my head, finally seeing things from his perspective. "Still...you stuck around to make sure we had a place to live. That wasn't selfish."

"Enough about sad things." He forced a smile. "We found your mother."

"You did?"

"She's in Canada with Hemsworth's sister," Dad said, relieved. "Once all of this is over, I'm going to get her myself."

When I heard him say that getting my mother back depended on all of this being over, my heart sank. How could I possibly tell them that it wasn't over—and it wouldn't be, ever—and it was all my fault. I wasn't strong enough to stand against them, and now they had what they needed. They had the whole journal.

"Are you hungry?" Dad asked. "Let's go get you something to eat." Dad stood and held up the curtain for me.

When I stepped out, everyone stopped what they were doing and looked at me.

Dad walked toward Dale's wife, who was opening a bag of ham and handed her an extra plate.

"It's good to have you back," Rashida said with a smile.

"Thanks." I looked around. "Where are Hugh and Sophia?"

Rashida glared at Victor, who was sitting next to her. "You didn't tell her?" she said in a hushed tone.

Victor shrugged. "Why do I always have to be the bearer of bad news?"

"Tell me what?" I pressed.

Rashida sighed then looked at me. "They left. Sophia couldn't handle being here with me, so...she left. And Hugh went with her."

"What?" I looked at Victor. "Where would they go?"

Victor shook his head. "No idea."

Unbelievable. "What about Hemsworth's briefcase?" I asked, trying to hold on to any sliver of hope.

Rashida opened her mouth but didn't seem sure how to say it. "There wasn't anything useful inside."

"What about Conor's phone?"

"All we know is they've re-built Fort Valley Island, and it seems to be their new headquarters now."

Dad came back holding a plate with a ham and cheese sandwich. "Here you go, sweetheart," he said, handing it to me.

"Thanks, Dad." I plopped down on the floor across from Victor and Rashida.

"We may have another plan," Victor said. "We can

expose them to the world. We can post everything online and let the people have a say."

"I'm sure the family of the soldiers will come forward and back us up," Rashida added. "Surely they've noticed the glitches."

"The only problem," Dad cut in, "is not being able to control how people will react to it. If they find out the government can't be trusted, it's over. It'll be like setting a wildfire, and we'll end up starting a rebellion."

"And that's if they believe us," Benji chimed in from the corner. "It could very well backfire on us. We're nothing but a small group who rebelled against the government. Who do you think they're gonna believe?"

There was a long pause, but then Rashida started, again. "We've been seriously considering going our separate ways—most likely overseas. Dale's wife already talked about going to Colombia. Benji was going to try London for a while."

"Wait, we never talked about that." Victor turned to Rashida almost offended. "We're not giving up."

Rashida shrugged. "We're at a dead end, Vic."

"We don't even have enough resources to stay here another week," Benji agreed, pointing to a small opening in the corner that led outside. "We're using the solar panels we took from the yacht, but it's not enough."

"Grace was nice enough to give us food and a key to the lodge for whenever we want to shower," Dad added. "But we can't expect her to keep supplying for us."

"Wait, what? Grace knows we're here?" Grace was not only Ethan's foster mother, but she pretty much raised Shawn and me as well. When our father was drinking his life away, she fed us and took care of us when we got sick. "She cannot be dragged into this."

"We asked her not to say anything," Victor said, raising his hands defensively. "I don't think she has."

"Still!" I stood, feeling the need to move around. My palms were starting to sweat. "Someone could've seen her, or…" Oh God, if anything happens to anyone else, I wouldn't be able to bear it.

"What did they do to you, M's?" Victor asked, and when I turned around, I caught him staring at my neck.

"Hey, guys?" Benji called out, looking up from his laptop. "I think the president just got shot."

"What?" Dad reached for Benji's laptop and turned it around for us to see. Everyone gathered around the screen with eyes unblinking. They watched as terror spread through the crowds and screams filled the air. Field agents swarmed the location, ordering everyone to stay down. The camera pointed to the hotel we had been at, and my heart instantly sank.

"It was the Order," I murmured, sitting back on the ground and forcing a bite out my sandwich. "They had it all planned out."

"Why would the Order want to kill the president?" Dad asked, puzzled.

"For the VP to take his position," I said. "They're all in it together."

Rashida shook her head, baffled. "Oh, this is bad."

"You have no idea," I mumbled.

"I say we ditch the country today," Victor said. "And I mean like…now. We should go while everything and everyone is in chaos."

"We're not going anywhere," I said, chewing. "It's only a matter of time before all of our faces are wanted for that assassination."

Dad looked horrified. "Why?"

"The room the shooter was in..." I pointed to the screen. "It was under my name."

"You knew this was gonna happen?" Victor asked, horrified. "Why didn't you tell us?"

"What difference would it make?" I shrugged. "We're screwed no matter what."

"So, this is the end?" Victor looked from me to Rashida. "They win?"

"Oh, it's not the end," I clarified, taking another bite of my sandwich. "Now that they have the whole journal...they're only getting started."

* * *

Later that night, I lay awake inside my hole while everyone else retreated to their own space.

"I am so sorry." I heard Rashida's voice whisper in the dark. "For killing your dad, I mean."

I pushed the sheet to the side and spotted her sitting by the water, next to Victor.

"You already told me about the dormant effect, babe." Victor nudged her. "Besides, the guy was a douche."

She buried her face in her hands. "Still..."

"Hey..." He pulled her close. "Enough about this, okay?"

Rashida reached for his hand. "I need you to promise me something."

"Anything."

"If I ever get caught," she said, "I need you to promise me that you will not come for me."

"I can't promise that."

"Victor, I'm serious." She looked him in the eyes. "I don't know that I can handle if anything happens to you."

"Why don't we talk about good things?" He smiled. "When all this is over, would you like to travel the world with me?"

She chuckled despite herself. "I'd like that."

Victor leaned in to kiss her, and I hid behind the sheet. Privacy was definitely a problem in that cave.

Rashida suddenly screamed, and I jumped out to see what had happened. Two men were surfacing from the water, but the cave was too dark to see their faces. One of them was strong and had on a soldier uniform while the other was thin and wore a suit. Victor reached for the taser gun, as did Dad.

"Stop right there!" Dad ordered while the tall man climbed up the rocks, pulling the other slim man with him. "I said, stop!"

Dale's wife clicked on the flashlight, and we all gasped at the sight of Ethan dragging the president out of the water, then throwing him on the ground.

CHAPTER 18

*E*THAN STARED at me as multiple lights pointed at his face.

"Mr. President!" Benji jumped to his feet. "We thought you were dead!"

"That was the plan," Ethan murmured, his eyes never leaving me.

"Come, Mr. President." Benji handed him a towel and guided him to the back of the cave. "We'll find something dry for you to wear."

"Who're you?" Victor asked, still pointing the gun at Ethan. "And how did you find us?"

Ethan walked past Victor, ignoring the gun, and headed toward me. Everyone fell silent as they watched. He dug his hand into the inside pocket of my jacket—his jacket.

"What are you…?"

He pulled out his phone then stepped back with an innocent look on his face.

I stared at him in disbelief. "You tracked me?"

"You just happen to take my phone," he said, turning

around. "But that's beside the point. Right now, we have to make sure the president stays safe."

"Who is this guy?" Victor murmured, looking at Rashida.

"That's Ethan," Rashida whispered to him. "Mia's husband."

Victor's mouth dropped open. "Come again?"

"Ethan." Dad brought him a towel. "Here you go, son. I'll get you some dry clothes, and you can change behind that curtain."

"Thank you, sir." Ethan took the towel and followed Dad to his corner of the cave. Meanwhile, Rashida went to talk to the president.

"M's..." Victor whispered, pulling me aside. "Is that guy really your husband?" I nodded as he looked at me, baffled. "You don't seem very excited that he's here."

I sighed. "It's a long story."

"What did he do to you?" he asked. "I can beat him up if you need me to. I don't care if he looks like the Hulk."

I chuckled despite myself.

"I'm just saying." He threw his arms up. "No one messes with my sister. Not on my watch."

"Forget Ethan." I pinched him on his side, and he jerked back. "What's up with you and Rashida?"

He offered a smug smile. "I told you she had the hots for me."

"How did that happen?"

"I'm not sure." He glanced over his shoulder at Rashida across the cave. "I don't know if she just felt bad for almost killing me, or for actually killing my dad. Somehow, in the end, it all worked out." He stopped and looked at me. "That sounded really bad. I gotta start practicing how I'm gonna tell our story to our kids."

I laughed. "I'm really happy for you both."

"She's amazing, M's."

"No!" The president yelled as he backed into a corner. "Get away from me!"

Rashida took another step toward the president. "Listen to me—"

"No!"

Victor rushed to Rashida's side while Ethan came to mine. "What's going on?" Ethan asked, his voice low.

"No idea," I whispered back.

Rashida reached for the laptop and turned on the live stream. "Look!" She turned the screen toward the president. "If he didn't want to assassinate you then why is he giving a speech confirming your death?"

The president stared at the news with his mouth hanging open. "Why should I believe you?"

"Because we saved your life, you ungrateful jerk!"

"Okay." Victor pulled Rashida back, and she huffed, frustrated. "Take a breath, sexy lady."

"Mr. President, sir." Dad chimed in. "If you allow us to please tell you what we know—"

"How much do you want?" the president asked, moving back like a cornered cat. "Just say the sum, and I'll pay."

Victor looked offended. "We didn't abduct you."

"Then, I'm free to go?"

Victor sighed. "No."

"Then, that's called abduction."

"We just want you to shut down the Catalyst trial," Rashida cut in.

The president turned to Rashida as if she was completely mental. "The what trial?"

Ethan rolled his eyes. "Oh, boy. This is going to be a long night." He held up a towel as he turned to face me. "So, your dad said you know a place I can shower?"

It was dark outside with only the moon lighting our way. I started down the familiar trail and was surprised I didn't have to bite back tears as I walked Ethan to the lodge.

"Sorry for just showing up here," Ethan said, following close behind. "I wasn't sure what else to do with the president. I was hoping the opposition would have a plan."

"What is their end game?" I asked.

"All I know is that Conor has taken the president of China to a safe place."

"Where is that?"

Ethan shrugged. "They never told me."

After entering the lodge, we kept the lights off so as not to call undue attention. The moon was shining extra bright, and it bathed the wooden walls and floors, giving just enough glow.

"Bathroom is the first door on your right," I said, pointing the flashlight to the end of the hall. "I'll keep a lookout until you're done."

Ethan nodded. "Thanks."

Once the shower turned on, I waited a few minutes then pushed the door open and peeked inside. "I'm going to put your wet clothes in the drier," I said, picking up his clothes from the floor. "It should be done by the time you get out."

"Okay."

I rushed out of the bathroom and leaned my back against the closed door. I pressed my eyes shut and sucked in a deep breath. It took every ounce of self-control for me not to get into that shower with him.

After he was done, he walked out with a towel wrapped around his waist and a dark green stone necklace hanging down his neck. I had to rip my eyes off of him. He stood by the laundry door and saw that the dryer was still running.

"Sorry. I didn't think it was gonna take this long to dry, but your camo pants are pretty thick."

"That's alright." He leaned on the door. "Have you showered?"

"Not yet."

"Then, go ahead. I'll wait for my clothes."

I walked past him, and his chest brushed my shoulder. I slowed my pace trying to pathetically prolong our contact, but then his arm stretched out in front of me and I stopped.

"This..." he whispered as he reached for my left hand. He rubbed his thumb gently over my tattoo, and my heart began to race. "Still means something to me."

I closed my eyes and squeezed his hand. It was still warm from the hot shower, and the scent of fresh soap filled the air between us. I wanted him so bad, and I'm sure he could feel it.

"I can't," I choked.

He dropped his arm and pulled back. I escaped into the bathroom with my skin on fire. If he held me in that laundry room for another second, I wouldn't be able to resist him any longer.

After the shower, I walked out rubbing a towel on my

damped hair. As I made my way to the lobby, Ethan threw the magazine aside and stood from the sofa. After throwing the towel in the hamper, I locked the front door, and we started our way back.

As I skipped down the steps, I suddenly noticed that Ethan had stopped. I turned around and spotted him staring into the woods.

"Ethan?"

"What is that?" he asked, focused on something in the darkness. It wasn't until I followed his gaze that I noticed what he was staring at.

"It's a tire swing," I said.

"I know that." He took a step toward it. "Does it mean anything…to us?"

"No." I lied. "Now, let's go. We have to get back to the cave."

He grunted then grabbed his head. Another surge. He bent over and leaned against a tree. I sighed when I realized he was standing where Shawn caught us kissing. And close enough to the spot where I said I loved him for the first time.

"I'm sorry." Ethan raised a hand toward me. "I'll be right there."

I hugged my arms, trying to hold myself together. "It's okay. I know how sharp those surges can be."

He stood straight and sucked in a deep breath. "I'm good." He walked past me without even making eye contact. He looked upset. Okay, so I lied. The swing did mean something. It was our meeting spot all through that summer, and surely he remembered it. I wish he hadn't.

Those surges were too dangerous. He could have a seizure so strong, he would never recover.

The rest of the walk back was silent with only crickets and frogs in the distance. The moon was bright above us, and it reflected against the water as we stopped in front of the waterfall.

"Before we go inside..." Ethan turned to face me. "I want to give you something." He pulled the necklace over his head and held out his open hand with the dark green stone in it.

"What is it?" I asked, reaching to touch it.

"Your brother's ashes."

I looked up at him, shocked.

"I took Shawn's body to the base's morgue," he said, his voice barely audible, "and asked a friend to have him cremated and made into this."

I looked down at the stone again, and my eyes began to sting. Ethan opened my hand and placed it gently in it. "I won't ever find the words—"

"You don't have to ask me for forgiveness, Ethan."

"I'm not. I can't ever ask you for that. I don't deserve it." He paused and turned toward the waterfall. "You should go inside."

"You're not coming?"

"I don't want to make this any harder for you, Mia."

"Ethan..." I stepped in front of him. "I could tell the moment you pulled that trigger that it wasn't you—"

"I pulled the trigger," he hissed, digging his finger into his own chest. "I shot my best friend. I killed him."

I grabbed his face and looked into his eyes. "You're gonna have to forgive yourself."

He ripped himself from my grip, all the while shaking his head. "I can't do that."

"Ethan, please—"

"You should go inside."

"Where will you go?"

"I don't know, yet."

"Then at least wait to hear what the plan is," I said with my heart aching. "We may need your help."

He didn't respond, and for as long as he was quiet, I couldn't breathe. Why couldn't I let him go? After all, I had left him behind in the cabin for his own good. But as he stood in front of me, I couldn't do it again. It felt too excruciating.

"Fine," he said and my heart felt suddenly lighter. I knew the best thing for him would be to get as far away from me as possible, but I also knew that the moment he left, he would rip the heart right out of my chest.

* * *

As soon as we walked back inside Victor yelled, "About time!" and everyone turned around to look at us.

"What's going on?" I asked.

Dad sighed. "He still doesn't believe us."

"That idiot," Rashida pointed at the president who was then tied with his hands behind his back, "had the audacity to accuse us of being the ones who plotted to kill him! Can you believe it?"

"They have been telling me for months about this group called the opposition," the president mumbled to himself. "They warned me you all had sent threats."

Rashida threw her arms in the air, exasperated. "Somebody please shut him up!"

Victor took a duct tape from inside his backpack and taped the president's mouth shut. "Sorry your highness, but my lady is the boss here."

"Now what?" Rashida rested her hands on her hips. "Our only hope is in the hands of a moron! You know what? No, scratch that. I'm the moron because I actually voted for him!"

Dale's wife looked like she was about to cry. Benji stared blankly at the floor as if there was nothing else he could do. Dad walked away from the group and sank into a corner, holding his head in his hands, utterly defeated. I sat next to him, trying to tune out Rashida's unending complaints.

"This is it," Dad said, lifting his head and looking in the president's direction. "This was our only hope. He was our only hope."

"There's gotta be something else," I said.

Dad looked at me and forced a smile. "Since when did you become so optimistic?"

"It's not optimism," I said, glancing at Ethan who was lying across the cave with a backpack as a pillow. "It's revenge."

"Do you have a plan in mind?"

"More like a Hail Mary," I said, keeping my voice low. "But you have to promise me something."

He nodded. "Anything."

I looked around to make sure no one was listening. "As soon as you get access to a Catalyst machine, I need you to put Ethan through it and erase his memory again."

"Why would you...?"

"He shouldn't have to live the life the Order chose for him." He shouldn't continue to be the killer they created. "It's not fair."

"But what about you?"

"It's best if he doesn't remember me," I said pushing through the knot in my throat. "We can't be together, anyway."

"Mia—"

"Promise me, Dad." I looked him in the eyes. "Please?"

He nodded, hesitantly. "Okay."

"Thank you."

He let out a long exhale. "So, what's this Hail Mary you're thinking about?"

CHAPTER 19

THE FOLLOWING DAY, after Victor and Rashida came back from the lodge, they brought with them a bag full of food. It was almost lunchtime, and we were all starving.

"Where did you find it?" I asked, looking through one of the bags while Ethan reached in for the beef jerky.

"It was in the lobby of the lodge," Victor said, handing the cold cuts over to Dale's wife who already had the bread.

"I bet it was Grace," Dad said. "Bless her heart."

"Who's Grace?" Ethan asked with his mouth full of jerky.

Grace was Ethan's adopted Mom, and Dad looked at me. I shook my head. "Just an old friend," Dad said, turning his attention back to the bag. "Wonderful person."

Ethan nodded without any further thought, then offered the president a piece of bread. "Can anyone cut him loose so he can eat?" Ethan asked.

Rashida rolled her eyes. "Fine, but if he does anything stupid, it's on you."

"Sure, put it on my tab."

Victor laughed, and Rashida glared at him. "What? I didn't know Hulk had a sense of humor."

Rashida gladly ripped the duct tape from the president's face, and he grimaced. "Where is my suit?" he demanded while Victor reached over his back to cut his hands loose.

"It's on a rock outside. It should be dry by now," Benji said, innocently.

"Can I have it back?" the president asked, though sounding more like a demand. "It's a Brioni Vanquish."

"Brioni, who?" Victor teased, walking back in with the suit. "I think the sun shriveled it up a bit but, oh well, gives it more character."

He ripped the suit from Victor's hand then sat back down. "You all are going to pay for this."

"Here, catch!" Ethan tossed him a loaf of bread, and although he looked like he wanted to scarf it down like a caveman, he took small bites. Ethan rolled a bottle of water to the president's feet, and he gulped it down before he was even done chewing.

"Hey, guys?" Benji's voice came from across the cave. "Come check this out."

We all turned and saw Benji peering into his laptop's screen. Dale's wife was sitting a few feet behind him with her eyes wide open.

Benji propped up his laptop on top of a towel on a rock and sat back to watch the president of China as he spoke from a podium. He was speaking in Chinese, but there was an English voice-over interpreting in the background, along with English subtitles.

"Did he just admit defeat?" Rashida jumped to her feet and rushed to watch. She leaned over and pressed the button to raise the volume.

I stood, and Ethan followed. We walked over just enough where we could see the screen.

Victor went to stand next to Rashida. "What's going on, babe?"

"Aren't you listening to this nonsense?" Rashida threw her hands in the air in another wave of frustration. "He's saying that the Chinese government is merging with the U.S. and...wait, what? Together they will make the world a better place?"

Dad stood and walked over to Dale's wife, who looked hypnotized. "Anne?" He waved a hand in front of her face, but she didn't respond. Her eyes were wide open, staring at the screen. "Oh, no!" Dad turned around with an urgent cry. "Mia, don't look!" His hands were in front of my face, blocking my view of the screen. He then grabbed me by my shoulders and turned me around. He gave Ethan a pleading look and Ethan turned away, too.

"What's going on?" I asked. Dad looked horrified. "Dad?"

"This is not just a news report," he said, his voice barely audible. "This is the Catalyst." His eyes shifted back to Anne; still hypnotized by the screen.

I looked back at Dad, fear washing over me. "The mind control?"

Dad nodded.

"Wait, what's going?" Victor asked, confused. "What's wrong with Dale's wife?"

Rashida and Benji looked at Archer, waiting for him to explain. He opened his mouth, but nothing came out.

"Spill it, Archer." Rashida barked, impatiently. "What's going on?"

Dad turned to Rashida. "You know how the Catalyst machine works, right?"

"Yeah?"

"They're using the same algorithm with the pixels in the screen," he explained. "Everything that's said with the Catalyst algorithm running in the background…" His eyes shifted to Dale's wife, again. "It's creating a simulation to manipulate the brain into believing that's true."

Rashida stared at Archer, mortified. "You mean like…brainwashing?"

"Exactly."

Victor looked back at the screen, confused. "Why aren't we all stoned-faced like her?" he asked, pointing to Anne.

"We have the mind-lock," Archer replied. "Mia and Ethan, don't. And neither does the president."

We turned to look at him. He was quiet in the corner, listening. Luckily, he couldn't see the screen from where he was sitting.

"But Dale's wife is deaf," Victor mumbled. "How come it's affecting her, she can't even hear what they're saying?"

"She read the subtitles," Archer said. "As long as she knows what's being said, it'll affect her."

"Oh, this is bad." Rashida started pacing around, shaking her head. "This is really bad."

"No…" Benji mumbled from the corner. "This is bad."

Everyone's eyes widened in shock, and I looked at Dad, again. "What's happening?"

Benji raised the volume, and I could hear the news report. "The Police Department would appreciate your cooperation in locating the following individuals who are wanted for the assassination of the president. Mia Hunter is on the loose and dangerous..." When everyone gasped, I was sure they had a picture of me on the screen. "She was seen at the Grand Hotel a few days ago, renting the exact room where the shot came from. We have reason to believe she had help from others. If you know the whereabouts of any person shown below, please notify the Police Department immediately."

When Rashida cursed and hurled the laptop against the wall, I knew they had shown all of our pictures. Dad melted to the floor, and so did Benji. Rashida walked away, shaking her head, and Victor followed after her.

"Maybe there's still a chance not everyone is gonna watch it," Benji said, desperate to find a silver-lining that simply did not exist.

"Very unlikely," Archer replied, rubbing his eyes. "If you heard that your country was merging powers with another, that's not a news report you would want to miss. I'm sure they'll keep replaying it to make sure everyone watches."

I looked up and caught Ethan staring at me. "So, now what?" he asked.

"Now..." I looked around at everybody. "We cross our fingers and hope our plan works."

"And if it doesn't?" Victor asked, doubt making his voice tremble. Rashida reached for his hand, knowing the answer.

"Then, that's it." There was no other way to describe it. "Game over."

* * *

I PICKED up Rashida's backpack and crouched next to Dad, handing him an envelope. "Here's a fake ID and a passport. Apparently, Rashida and Benji had it made back on the island in case we needed it. You might have to dye your hair darker, though. Also, don't shave. The rugged look helps disguise your face. It should at least help you get to Canada."

"I want to stay and help."

"No," I said, firmly. "The Order already knows you're the one who has Mom's memory. Once they realize there's a lot more about the Catalyst she didn't write down, they will come for you and who knows what they'll find."

"I don't like this." He huffed as he took the envelope. "Not one bit." He turned around and walked away just as Victor dropped his backpack on the ground next to me.

"All I wanted was to backpack around Europe, but no! I had to get involved in the family business."

I stood and reached to fix the collar of the camo jacket Ethan had let him borrow. "Be very careful out there, and whatever you do," I raised a finger of authority, "do not use your credit card. They're monitoring your dad's account."

"What difference will it make?"

"Victor, I'm serious."

"Fine." He threw his hands up. "I won't."

"You got everything you need?" I asked, pointing to his backpack. When he nodded, I picked it up and pushed it into his chest. "Then go say bye to Rashida and leave. We can't waste any more time."

"What if I can't find him?" Victor gulped, nervously.

"Then you did the best you could." I pulled him into a tight embrace. "I love you."

He tightened his arms around me. I pulled back, suppressing a stream of tears. "Now go. Get out of here."

* * *

IN LESS THAN AN HOUR, Ethan, Rashida and I were the only ones left in the cave.

"My word! How much longer until it's time to go?" Rashida grumbled as she glanced at her watch.

"Patience," Ethan murmured, lying on the ground with his eyes closed and his head on a backpack.

"What are you doing?" she snapped, irritated.

"Taking a nap," he replied as if that was the obvious thing to do in a time like that. "Who knows what's going to happen after today. Might as well sleep while you can."

"How do you expect to be walking around with me and not call attention?" the president called out from across the cave, his arms still behind his back.

"You know, that is a very valid point." Rashida glanced over her shoulder at him. "I guess we'll just have to disfigure your face so no one recognizes you!"

"Play nice," Ethan said, but Rashida shrugged carelessly.

"We are not the enemy, Mr. President. I really am sorry that you can't see that," I said as I glanced at my watch.

"You expect me to believe that a group of rebels is trying to save the world?"

"It does sound pretty stupid when you put it like that," Ethan admitted with a chuckle.

"The question you should be asking," I told him, "is why would your second in command confirm your death when clearly they didn't find your body?"

"They were trying to protect me," the president replied. "They probably wanted whoever tried to kill me, to think they succeeded."

"Oh, my God." Rashida shook her head in disbelief. "I can't believe I voted for this moron."

The sound of tree branches being snapped came from outside, and the three of us jumped to our feet.

"What was that?" Rashida asked, alarmed.

"Well, this moron has had enough of this game." The president stood tall and proud. He pulled his hands from his back which apparently weren't tied at all and held up Rashida's cell phone. "It's been a real pleasure spending time with you all, but I'm afraid it's over now."

"How did you get my phone?" Rashida asked, appalled.

"Your little boyfriend dropped it earlier," he said, shoving the phone into his pocket. At that, countless of field agents, along with the president's guards, rushed into the cave with their weapons drawn.

"Let me see your hands!" They barked, pointing their guns at us. We put our hands up and laid flat with our faces on the ground.

"Are you okay, Mr. President?" One of his guards rushed to his side. "Did they hurt you, sir?"

"You're making a mistake," I told the president as a field agent cuffed me. "They are going to kill you."

"Shut up!" The field agent yelled as he strip-searched us.

They pulled out our phones, threw it on the ground, and stepped on it.

"You are going to the station," a guard said pulling me with him, but a field agent got in his way.

"The girl will be coming with us," the field agent said.

"And why is that?" the guard challenged, shielding me.

The agent pointed his gun at the guard's face. "Not your business."

I glanced at the president, wondering when—or if—he was going to step in.

"I'm sure that won't be necessary," the president finally said, stepping forward. "Guns down, please." When one of the guards didn't obey, the president stepped in front of him. "Are you forgetting who's in charge?"

The guard traded glances with some of the others then lowered his weapon. "No, sir."

The president stepped back and took a deep breath. "Okay, then. All of the rebels will come with us, and that's final. Let's go."

We were escorted to an open field where there was a large military chopper waiting. More guards with guns jumped out of the helicopter and rushed to the president's side.

"I'm fine," the president assured each one of them. Some verbal, while others with a simple nod. "Strap them in."

We stumbled into the chopper only to be grabbed by our jackets and thrown onto the seat. My arm hurt as it stayed cuffed behind me.

"So much for our plan." Rashida snorted as the guard

buckled her up. "Hey! Do you like your hands, buddy? Then, keep it away from me."

I looked at the president as he sat across from me. "You should put on a bulletproof vest," I warned.

Ethan leaned his head back as if getting comfortable in his seat. "I would listen to her if I were you."

"Enough, all of you!" the president yelled, buckling himself in. "I've had enough with this nonsense."

Rashida leaned forward. "If you want to walk into your own slaughter, suit yourself, but at least have the decency of dropping us off somewhere."

He looked out the chopper as it began to ascend. "Careful what you wish for, darling."

Rashida shot a glance at me, peeved. "He did not just call me darling."

Ethan laughed.

I looked out the window, and despite knowing that we were headed straight to the lion's den, the sight of the waterfall from above was surprisingly peaceful. If that were the last image my mind ever recorded, I would be okay with that.

Ethan nudged me. "It's not over, yet."

"I don't know if I can go through it all, again."

"I won't let them hurt you," he promised. "Never again."

"They will most likely kill you before they get to me."

He shrugged. "I dare them to try."

I closed my eyes, trying to suppress the anxiety I felt rising inside me.

"Mia, look at me," Ethan said, firmly. "They haven't won, yet."

"Look around, Ethan. They've already won in so many ways."

Ethan reached for my hand which was still cuffed behind my back and squeezed it. I knew I shouldn't, but I gave in to his touch one last time.

* * *

As the chopper hovered above Fort Valley Island, I studied the president's expression. He kept looking down then around at his own guards with suspicion in his eyes. When our eyes finally locked, he rubbed the palms of his hands on his pants and took a deep breath. I could tell he was starting to believe us, and it might've been because he never actually told the pilot where to go, yet here we were. In a deserted island, in the middle of nowhere, meeting up with the same people that wanted all of us killed.

There were several yachts as well as other choppers, scattered all over the island. Some had flags from other countries such as Russia and India. I wondered if those presidents were also here, and had they already watched the Catalyst simulation video. Perhaps they were making their own, like the president of China had been manipulated to do.

Although being in Fort Valley should've given me a sense of dread, the familiarity filled me with a sense of calmness. That was the same cliff I'd jumped with my sister, and those were the same trees I'd trained with the group. If I were to die, I guess that wouldn't be the worse place in the world.

When the chopper landed, the wind was so strong it

felt like we were in the middle of a sandstorm. There were a lot more field agents than usual, and by the look on Rashida's face, I could tell she was noticing the same thing.

We were pushed out of the chopper then escorted by field agents up to the rocky hill. As we arrived at the newly remodeled entrance, a guard stopped us at the door. "We'll take them from here," he said.

The field agent stepped forward and pointed his gun at the guard's face. "We'll follow."

The guard hesitated but only for a moment. He opened the door and stepped aside to make way for all of us. The guards went ahead of us, while the field agents guarded our backs. I sucked in a deep breath, and Ethan's cuffed hands reached for mine. He gave it a light squeeze just as we appeared through the lobby.

Conor was standing by a small podium in front of a group of world leaders. Behind him was a large screen which if I had to guess was where they were going to play the simulation.

Conor signaled for someone else to take his place, then excused himself with a smile to his guests. My stomach twisted when Warren stood, and Sadykov followed. One of the agents pushed me to start walking again, and Ethan glared at him. We were led into a newly remodeled conference room. The smell of fresh paint still lingered in the air. Unlike the old office, this one had tall windows with thick burgundy curtains.

"What's going on here?" the president asked once the door shut behind us. "How come I was not informed of this meeting?"

"You were dead, Mr. President," Conor responded, walking around a brand new mahogany desk.

"This is not the type of meeting you arrange within a day or two," the President pressed, finally starting to sense something wasn't right.

"Sorry, what I meant to say was…" Conor pulled out a gun and pointed at the president. "You were supposed to be dead."

The president stepped back, but a field agent blocked the door. We were trapped, and I was not surprised.

"Moron," Rashida hissed under her breath.

Conor glanced at her. "Pardon me?"

"I wasn't talking to you," Rashida snapped. "Although, I can't say it doesn't also apply."

"Go back to the meeting," Sadykov stepped next to Conor. "We'll take care of them."

Warren stepped in front of me. "I gotta say, being inside your head is quite fascinating." He glanced at Ethan briefly then back at me. "Now I see why you risked so much to save him. Beautiful love story; truly breaks my heart to rip you two apart."

Ethan shoved himself between us, puffing out his chest.

"Well, well, well…" Warren smiled. "If it isn't the traitor. Do you know what we do to traitors?"

"Of course. I have done it for you."

"Ah, yes." Warren nodded. "So, then you know… when we put you through the Catalyst again, not only will we make you torture all of your new friends but also your own wife."

Ethan clenched his fists behind his back as his jaw

tightened. If he wasn't cuffed, and we weren't outnumbered, I'm sure he would've snapped Warren's neck.

"Why are you doing this?" the president asked Conor. "What do you want?"

"What does it look like?" Conor replied with an obvious expression. "I want your title and authority."

The president's mouth dropped open. He probably wasn't surprised by Conor's envy, but maybe what shocked him was how far Conor was willing to go to get it. "That room full of people already saw me. They know I'm not dead."

"That's alright." Conor wiggled the gun around the room. "I'll just blame it on one of these idiots. After all, they were the ones who plotted to kill you, right? I mean, that's what the news is saying."

"You're not going to get away with this," the president said in a firm tone.

"We'll see about that." Conor pointed the gun back toward his target again, and the president stepped back. A field agent who was standing behind Conor stepped forward, ever so slightly. He kept his head down, and I followed his movement. Something was different about him. When he looked up and our eyes locked, I had to hold back a gasp.

Seth!

He looked discreetly toward the window, and when I followed his gaze, I spotted half of Victor's face looking in through the glass. He was also disguised as a field agent. I turned my attention back to Seth. He clutched his gun and waited for my signal.

"It was an honor serving by your side, sir." Conor

continued. "I will make sure that you'll be remembered and honored in history as a hero to this country." The clicking of the gun echoed in the room, and I signaled to Seth with a discreet nod. Seth raised his weapon and shot Conor in the back. Gunshots threw all of us to the ground. Ethan fell on top of me, shielding me with his body as Victor blasted through the window along with Sophia, Hugh, and a small army of soldiers.

By the time I opened my eyes, all of the soldiers that were disguised as field agents were holding their guns to our enemy's heads.

I looked at Hugh. "I thought you'd left us."

Hugh smiled, holding a gun to one of the guard's head. "You know we wouldn't do that. Besides, I told you we needed more people on our side, and I told you about Seth from the very beginning."

"So when you sent Victor to find Seth, you had no idea we were gonna be with him?" Sophia asked as she removed my cuffs.

"No clue," I confessed. "I was just hoping to get enough back-up."

Sophia went on to uncuff Ethan then Rashida. The president stood with his eyes widened in shock. "How did you know they would bring us here?"

Ethan reached into the president's suit jacket and pulled out Rashida's phone. Victor held up another phone which he used to track it.

"You stripped us but not yourself, sir," Ethan noted as he tossed Rashida back her phone.

"You're welcome," Rashida said to the president while rubbing her sore wrists.

"This was your plan all along?" the president asked, looking at me. "How in the world did you know it would work?"

"All I knew was that as soon as they found you, they would make sure to have you brought to them to finish what they started. And if we just happen to be with you..." I looked at Warren. "The famous Trojan horse, I guess."

Warren applauded. "Bravo." He bowed in front of me, mockingly.

"It's over, Warren."

He glanced up with a devilish smile. "You're absolutely right."

He lunged toward me, and I felt a sharp stab in my stomach. When my eyes locked with his, he yanked the knife out, and Ethan tackled him to the floor.

Sophia gasped as I dropped to my knees. She rushed to my side while Ethan kept punching Warren in the face. I couldn't breathe, and I clung to Sophia's arm.

She screamed, horrified.

Ethan stopped, leaving Warren unconscious on the floor. He rushed to catch me before my head hit the ground and laid me gently on the floor. I choke as blood splattered out of my mouth.

"Hey, it's okay," he whispered, ripping off his sleeve and applying pressure to my wound. "You're gonna be okay, you hear me?"

My head dropped to the side, and my eyes fell on Sadykov. He lifted his lips vengefully then looked down at Conor's gun which was by his feet.

No! I wanted to yell, but nothing came out except small

bursts of gasps. I coughed as I watched in horror as Sadykov kicked up the gun and aimed at Victor's chest.

* * *

THE LONELY LIGHT of morning penetrated through the thin fabric of the curtain while the smell of medicine filled the air. A machine beeped on the side of my bed while a bag of IV hung down a metal hook.

Ethan looked up from the magazine, and when our eyes met, he jumped up in surprise.

"Hey!" He kept his voice low and soft as he reached for my hand. "There you are."

"What happened?" I asked, pushing through my dry throat.

Ethan leaned closer and peered his soft blue eyes into mine. "It's over, my love," he said softly as he caressed my hair. "You don't have to run anymore."

"It's over?" I echoed, letting out a sigh of relief as an overwhelming sense of liberation washed over me. "Is it really over?" My voice cracked and all of the tears I'd been holding for months came rushing back.

Ethan kept wiping them, but it was useless. I started to sob, and he pulled me into a strong embrace, shushing me and rocking me back and forth without even caring that I was drenching his shirt.

"Wait…" I pushed him away. "You can't be here."

"It's okay—"

"No, it's not okay."

"Mia—"

"We already talked about this, Ethan."

"Talked about what?" He looked at me puzzled, but then Dad appeared and put a hand on his shoulder.

"Can you give us a minute, son?"

Ethan nodded, squeezing my hand before leaving. Dad smiled as he pulled up a chair and sat next to me.

"Is it really over?" I asked, wiping my face.

"Yes, it is." Dad smiled. "That Hail Mary worked like a charm."

I closed my eyes and let out the longest breath of relief.

"There is something else you should know," Dad added, and I turned to look at him. "Remember how you asked me to put Ethan through the Catalyst again?"

I pushed myself to sit up. "Yeah?"

"Well, I did."

I stared at him, confused. "Dad, he was just here. He remembered me."

"That's because I inserted your old memories into his mind." He offered a smile. "Benji still had your disk."

I opened my mouth to speak, but nothing came out. I was speechless. Ethan had my memories inside his mind? I wasn't sure whether to feel happy or terrified.

"I took your mother's memories, remember? It worked for me. So, I figured it would probably work for him, too."

"What exactly does he remember?"

"Pretty much everything before Hugh put you through the Catalyst the first time," he explained. "However, seeing that you got stabbed and put into a coma, we did have to catch him up on a lot of other things."

"Does he remember..." I could feel my voice shaking, "working for the Order?"

Killing Shawn?

"No. But he's been asking questions so you should start thinking about what you would like him to know."

I leaned forward and gave my dad the tightest hug. "How could I ever thank you?"

He shook his head. "You gave me my wife back. If anything, I'm the one who will forever be indebted to you."

"Mom's here?" I pulled back, suddenly excited. "Did you give her memories back? Did she remember you?"

He frowned as his shoulders sagged. "She hasn't responded, yet. But it's still too soon. It's only been three weeks—"

"Wait..." I leaned back, shaking my head. "I've been out for three weeks?"

"You've woken up here and there, but you were pretty out of it." He rubbed his tired eyes then ran his fingers through his gray hair. "The doctor said you were struck with extreme exhaustion and dehydration and your body needed to rest."

"Oh, God!" I clutched to his arm. "Victor! How's Victor?"

"Look who it is!" Victor walked in holding a foam coffee cup. "If it isn't sleeping beauty."

Sophia walked in behind him and slapped the back of his head. "Keep your voice down, you dork."

"Why? She's awake."

"Still, she could have a headache or something."

They both stopped and stood at the foot of my bed. "How are ya, sis?" Victor asked, sitting on the edge of the bed.

"Me?" I asked, terrified and relieved at the same time.

"You're the one who got shot!" Victor lowered his head, and I looked at Sophia. "What?"

"Actually, Rashida got shot. She jumped in front of him," Sophia said. "She's still in the ICU."

"Oh, Victor." I wanted to hold his hand, but I couldn't reach. "I am so sorry."

Victor waved it off. "She'll be fine. She's a tough cookie."

Dad stood. "I'm gonna go check on her, see if there's an update."

Victor raised his coffee in gratitude and Dad offered him a small smile before walking out.

"So, how you feeling?" Victor asked. "Ready for a paintball match any time soon?"

I touched my wound and winced. "It's not 100%, but I should be able to take you on just fine."

"As weird as this whole thing is..." Victor turned to look at Sophia then back at me. "It's pretty cool."

"What is?" Sophia asked.

"The three of us," Victor said as if it should've been obvious. "Being family and all."

"Oh, thank God!" Hugh let out a breath as he walked in with a fast food bag in his hand.

"Ditto, bro!" Victor stood and snatched the bag from Hugh's hand. "I'm starving!"

Sophia tugged at Victor's arm. "Let's go eat outside."

"Why?"

She glared at him. "Because Mia is on a liquid diet, you moron." She snatched the bag from his hand and pushed him toward the door. "Let's go."

Hugh laughed as he sat at the foot of my bed. "Those

two have been terrified for days," he said reaching for my hand. "Don't ever scare us like that again, you hear me?"

"I'll try my best."

He smiled.

"So, what happened to them?" I asked, suddenly serious.

"The president allowed us to put the Order through the Catalyst before sentencing them to life in prison." He let out a breath of relief. "They won't know to come for us, ever again."

"What about the Catalyst trial?" I asked, curious.

"All of the laboratories have been confiscated and the Catalyst machines, destroyed. Well, except for one, and it's being used only to remove the military training from the soldiers."

"What about their memories?" I asked.

"There's no way to restore them. The war is over, and the trial has been shut down. That's the best we can do." Hugh sighed. "They'll just have to learn to live with everything else."

"What about the glitches and the surges?"

"The only ones who will have to worry about the dormant effect is you and Ethan. We already removed the military training from Rashida's mind," Hugh explained. "As for the surges, like I said… there's nothing we can do for them, anymore. Our only other option is to hope your Mom snaps back and figures out a way to fix it."

I nodded. "I guess it's still good news that the war is over, right?"

"Actually…" Hugh scooted closer to me and squeezed my hand. "I have some better news."

"Okay?"

"I'm planning on proposing to Sophia." He pulled out a small burgundy box from his pocket and opened it. "It was my mother's."

I touched the diamond ring with the tip of my finger. "She's going to love it."

"You think so?"

I shot a glance at him. "I'm sure by now she would take a rubber band if it meant finally being with you."

He laughed as he closed the box. "I'm glad you're finally awake because I didn't want to propose without you."

"Why is that?"

"Well..." He smiled. "I kinda need a best man."

I laughed and pulled him into a hug. "It would be my honor."

"Mia!" The kids stormed into the room. Hugh laughed as he was shoved out of the way. He stepped back and stood next to Ethan, who'd followed behind Sienna and Cody.

"She's all yours." Hugh chuckled as they tapped each other on the back. Ethan leaned against the wall and smiled at the sight of the kids climbing up my bed.

"Hey, guys!" I took Sienna in my arms then reached out to Cody, who was pouting at my feet. "What's up, buddy?"

"He's mad at you," Sienna said, snuggling beside me. "He thinks you left us."

I looked at Cody. "You know I would never do that."

He crossed his arms, upset. "But you did."

Ethan picked him up effortlessly and sat him between us. "She got sick, kiddo. That's why she had to leave for a little while. But she's better now."

Cody looked at me. "So, you won't leave anymore?"

I shook my head. "Never again."

He leaped forward and squeezed his little arms around me. Ethan laughed as he rubbed his little back.

"Don't ever leave us again, okay?" Cody's voice cracked, and he started to cry. Sienna leaned in and hugged him, too.

I looked at Ethan, and he smiled. "There's one more thing," he said, holding my gaze. "The doctor said that...the baby is fine."

The baby?

Ethan's grin grew wider. "A few weeks."

"Weeks?" The memory came back, slowly. The cabin in the mountains.

I couldn't believe it. The Order was gone. The Cata-lyst Trial was over. I looked down at the kids who had fallen asleep on my lap, and it was so unreal how my life was finally coming together.

Ethan laid on the bed and wrapped me in his strong arms. "I love you so much," he whispered, pressing his lips to my forehead. It was warm and comforting.

"I love you, too." I wanted to cry. "Always."

EPILOGUE

THE HEMSWORTH'S backyard couldn't have been more stunningly decorated. The wind brushed softly through the October morning as the sun shone brightly in the cloudless sky.

Sophia purposely waited to have her wedding in the fall because of how beautiful the leaves changed. Some trees had a stunning golden color, from a light brown to fiery orange. Others even turned yellow, but still blended beautifully with everything.

I skipped down the steps wearing none other than the latest Hemsworth heels and custom made best man's dress.

"Is she ready?" Victor asked, stopping in front of me and stretching out his neck for me to fix his tie.

"Not yet," I said, readjusting his knot.

"Mia?" a woman's voice came from behind me, and I turned around.

"Bonnie!" She smiled a sad smile, and I leaned in to hug her. "I'm so glad you could make it."

The baby, who was now almost two, reached for one of my earrings and squealed.

"No, Cole." Bonnie grabbed his little hand. "You can't grab that."

He looked up at his mom like he had no idea what she was saying, then threw himself toward my earring, again. His tiny fingers brushing against it as he giggled.

"Hi, Cole." His eyes widened in excitement when I let him take my silver hoop. "You like shiny things?" He squealed, opening his mouth wide, ready to shove it into his mouth. "Okay. Not a good idea, buddy."

Cole laughed, and I was instantly in love.

"Shawny..." Bonnie stepped aside, allowing for the ten-year-old to come out from behind her. "Say hi to your aunt, Mia."

When he timidly smiled at me, my eyes teared up. He looked just like Shawn—from the color of his hair to the shape of his nose.

"Hi," he said, timidly.

"Have you seen the chocolate fountain, yet?" I asked, and his eyes lit up.

"There's a chocolate fountain?"

I called Sienna and Cody over, and they sprinted in a competition of who would get to me first. "Guys, this is your cousin Shawn. Why don't you go show him the chocolate fountain?"

Meanwhile, Cole was slobbering all over my necklace.

"Cole, stop that." Bonnie pulled him away. "Sorry. He's at that phase, unfortunately."

"It's fine. Actually, I want you to have this." I pulled the necklace over my head and slipped it over hers. Cole's eyes widened in excitement, and within a second, the stone was right back in his mouth.

"What is it?" Bonnie asked, removing the stone from Cole's mouth and examining it.

"It's..." I wasn't sure how to say it. "It's uh..." I cleared my throat, hoping not to cry. "Shawn's ashes."

She looked up surprised, and her eyes immediately began to water. She opened her mouth to speak, but nothing came out. She stared down at the stone again, but this time with endearment and longing.

"I am so sorry." I touched her shoulder lightly. "We were offered a very generous compensation for everything we were put through, and I want you and the kids to take it."

"Mia..."

"I made Shawn a promise," I said. "Please let me keep it."

She nodded, suppressing her emotions. "Thank you." She leaned in and gave me a tight hug. "You're welcome to visit the boys any time."

"I sure will."

"Okay!" Sophia announced from the top of the stairs. She held onto the railing and took a deep breath. "I'm ready."

"Go ahead." Bonnie wiped the tears from her cheeks and smiled. "Duty calls."

* * *

OUTSIDE, I took my position as the best man, next to Hugh. "Ready?"

He took a deep breath as the music started, but stopped

breathing when he spotted Sophia through the double doors.

She ambled down the aisle in the center of hundreds of rows of family and friends. Hugh stood under a white gazebo by the lake, staring at her with a sparkle in his eyes.

"Breathe," I reminded him. "I'm not carrying you if you faint."

He chuckled and sucked in another deep breath. Sophia smiled, with Victor at her side.

When Hugh finally took Sophia by the hand, Victor came to stand next to me. "Being maid of honor is way cooler than best man," he whispered, nudging me with his shoulder.

I nudged him back. "You wish."

Their vows were simple but more meaningful than any couple I'd seen. They didn't have to say a lot to show they'd known each other all their lives, and loved each other for just as long. It was elegant yet simple, the perfect combination of their personalities.

Mom was sitting in the front row with Dad, but she wasn't looking at Sophia. She was blindly staring at the lake behind them as if she wasn't present, at all.

Ethan was sitting next to her holding our newborn, Ella, all the while bribing Cody to sit still. Sienna was never a problem, she looked so enchanted by Sophia's wedding dress, she wasn't even blinking. Cody looked adorable with his little Hemsworth bowtie and his gelled blonde hair glistening in the sun. He spotted me watching him and offered me two thumbs up. I laughed and looked at Ethan. He smiled then mouthed I love you to me. I still couldn't believe we not only had a baby, but also adopted the kids as our own.

I love you, too, I mouthed back.

After the ceremony was over, Sophia and Hugh turned toward us.

"Finally!" Victor wrapped Hugh in a bear hug, lifting him off the ground.

"Don't break the groom." Sophia slapped her brother. "I need him for the honeymoon."

"Oh, ew!" Victor put Hugh back on the ground. "T.M.I, Sis."

Sophia laughed, then turned to me. "I'm going to put this house up for sale."

"You're leaving Cooper Creek?"

She nodded. "We need to start fresh. There are too many bad memories here."

"Why don't you come to California?"

"No, thank you," she laughed, leaving out the fact that she would never be caught dead in a place as ghetto as Bunker Hill. "Besides, I reopened the boutique in the city and Hugh already requested the transfer. So, we'll see how that goes for the time being."

"Well, if you change your mind, our house is almost done. And we added a couple of extra bedrooms for when you both decide to visit."

"Oh, that we'll definitely do." She looked over her shoulder and leaned in as if about to tell me a secret. "No way I'm letting Victor be the favorite Uncle!"

I laughed.

"Why you always talking trash behind my back?" Victor snorted as he approached with an arm around Rashida.

"Congratulations!" Rashida leaned in and gave Sophia a hug. "You look absolutely gorgeous, by the way."

"Thank you," Sophia smiled, holding back the urge to model a little. "Let me know when you guys get hitched, and I'll make you an even better one."

"Sounds like a plan."

"So, you guys in good terms, now?" I asked, looking back and forth from Sophia to Rashida.

"She took a bullet for my brother. What can I say?" Sophia shrugged. "Well, we're going to greet the rest of the guests, but we'll see you all later."

Sophia pulled Hugh with her while Rashida and Victor turned to face me.

"Congratulations, Mama!" Rashida gave me a hug. "Sorry, we couldn't make it back for the birth of the baby."

"Oh, don't worry about it. I'm sure backpacking around the world was a lot more fun. Besides, when Ella was born, I was so tired I didn't want to see anybody, anyway."

Rashida laughed. "How do the boobs feel?"

"Okay, can we not go there?" Victor interjected with a gross look on his face.

Rashida laughed. "Fine, how old is the baby, now?"

"Four weeks."

"Wait a minute? Does that mean she was conceived while you were being held captive by the Order?" she asked in a low tone.

"No wonder it took you so long to escape. What? I'm just saying."

"So, where to next?" I asked.

"We haven't decided, yet. But it's between Hawaii and Cayman Island."

Victor rolled his eyes. "And you would think, after all we've been through, she would be sick of islands."

"Oh, wait!" Rashida clutched to Victor's arm, enthused. "Did you tell her, yet?"

"No, I was waiting for you."

Rashida turned to me with a grin. "Guess what? We got matching tattoos!"

Victor loosened his tie then unbuttoned his collar. "Check this out, M's." He pulled his shirt down, exposing the skin just below the right shoulder which said: I'm bulletproof.

Rashida pulled her dress, exposing the scar from the bullet she took also by her shoulder, and it said: I'm not!

"Get it?" They both blurted out into laughter, and Ethan gave me a quizzical look as he approached.

"There is my princess!" Victor grabbed Ella from Ethan's arms. "Come with Uncle Vic. Let's go light up fireworks for Auntie Sophia."

Ethan gave Rashida a pleading look, and she nodded. "Don't worry, he's not taking the baby anywhere near fireworks."

Ethan nodded. "Thank you."

Once Rashida walked away, Ethan pulled me to the dance floor. "You look stunning in that dress, by the way."

"I look fat."

"Stunning, nonetheless."

I slapped his arm, and he laughed. "Where are the kids?"

"Where do you think?" He turned toward the chocolate fountain. "We should be stricter with them now that we're parents."

"That sounds so weird," I chuckled.

"Not the word I was thinking of, but okay."

"You know what I mean." I wrapped my arms around his neck. "I can't believe we're parents."

He kissed my forehead. "How does it feel?"

"Complete."

"May I?" Dad asked, and Ethan stepped aside with a respectful nod. Dad spun me around then pulled me close.

"I had no idea you knew how to dance," I said.

"I was young once."

"I'm sorry I didn't invite you to my wedding."

He smiled. "I'm sure you looked just as beautiful as your mother did at our wedding."

"I don't think anyone could be as beautiful as her," I said, glancing to where she was sitting, by the lake. "How is she doing?"

He smiled a sad smile. "I'm just glad to have her back in my life."

"She still doesn't remember anything?"

"Not yet."

"Is it okay if I go sit with her for a bit?" I asked, and he pressed his lips to my forehead.

"We'll finish our father-daughter dance another time."

I gave him a tight hug, then started toward Mom. She stared out to the far end of the lake. The smell of wet grass though strong didn't seem to bother her. I crouched down in front of her wheelchair, but there was not even the slightest sign of recognition.

"Hi, Mom." It still felt strange saying those words aloud. "Sorry I haven't come around to see you lately, but I had a baby." I smiled, trying to ignore her aloofness. "Her name is Ella Grey, and she's beautiful. She's four weeks old today." I reached for her hand. "I can bring her later if you would like to hold her for a little bit?" I paused, but she didn't respond. "Also, I wanted to give you something."

I pulled Shawn's necklace over my head—the emerald Mom had given him when we were young—and the gem sparked in the sun. As the necklace swung in front of her face, her eyes caught the emerald, and she snapped out of it. Her eyes followed the stone as I put the necklace on her neck.

"I'm sure Shawn would've liked for you to have it back."

She looked at me, suddenly present. "Shawn?" she spoke softly, and my heart began to race.

"Yes, Shawn." My eyes filled with tears as she stared into them. "He kept your necklace all these years, and he loved you so much."

She brushed my face with the tip of her fingers. "Mia?" Her voice was barely above a whisper, and I leaned forward, eagerly.

"You remember me?"

"Of course I do," she smiled, softly, "my beautiful girl."

THE END

* * *

IF YOU HAVEN'T ALREADY and would like to read Mia's backstory in its entirety--as well as Mia and Ethan's love story and how it all began--Grab a copy of MEMORIES RECALLED today!

ALSO BY JESSIE CAL

Trouble in Love Series
My Best Friend and My Odd Side Job
My Best Friend and the Honeymoon Game
To All Characters I've Killed Before
My Ex and his List of Demands
My Ex and Our Pretend Proposal
And more…

Disarray Series
Memories Lost
Memories Restored
Memories Recalled
…also in audiobook

Anomalous Series
Secret Dreamer
Silent Healer
Opposing Forces
and more...
…also in audiobook

Fairytales Reimagined
Queen of Snow

Red Arrows

Beastly Secrets

Pure as Snow

Above the Sea

Heart of Glass

Upon a Dream

Tower of Gold

...also in audiobook

CONNECT WITH JESSIE

Sign up to her newsletter at jessiecalauthor.com
for weekly updates.

Follow her on Instagram
for daily laughs and teasers.

Follow her on BookBub
for new release alerts.

Follow her on Goodreads
to review her books

ABOUT THE AUTHOR

USA Today Bestselling author Jessie Cal has written over eighteen romance and suspense novels. Her books are known for their drama, romance, twists and turns, and passion that gives you all the feels.

Jessie lives in a small southern town with her hubby. When she's not visiting family, getting together with friends, or cuddling with a book, she's writing her next novel.

instagram.com/jessiecal_author